He opened his mind, trying to banish all irrelevant thought as he stared at Olana. He was an open receptacle, a receiving station for her emotional broadcast, her feelings, her thoughts. She raised her head reluctantly.

Olana . . . glowed.

Runner could feel her psychic presence. He wanted her. He needed her.

His hand reached for Olana, trembling . . . he fought the urge to paw the floor with cloven feet, to throw back his head and howl at the moon. She was strong . . . he knew he was melting in the glow of Olana's psychic heat . . . Runner fought her power.

Time passed, time moved, the night died.

The Night Runner: The Gemini Run

By

MICHAEL KERR

CHARTER
NEW YORK

A DIVISION OF CHARTER COMMUNICATIONS INC.
A GROSSET & DUNLAP COMPANY

THE GEMINI RUN

Copyright © 1979 by Robert Hoskins

Charter Books
A Division of Charter Communications Inc.
A Grosset & Dunlap Company
360 Park Avenue South
New York, New York 10010

2 4 6 8 0 9 7 5 3 1
Manufactured in the United States of America

*To Quinn,
a true Renaissance person,
with thanks*

ONE

The burly man sat in the stolen car, burrowed into a nest of his own clothing. Outside, in the November night, chilled rain fell steadily. It had been raining since early afternoon. Now, after midnight, the rain haloed street lights and filmed streets and sidewalks in ten thousand towns across New England.

"Damn it, I'm friggin' freezin'!"

The burly man's breath was visible as he cursed. His gloved fingers played with a cheap lighter, but his eyes were fixed, staring through the rain-streaked windshield. A single window was lit on the second floor of the Queen Anne-style house on the corner: a window in a spired tower that reached for the sky, expressing the soaring Victorian ambitions of the house's builder. Both ambitions and builder were eighty years dead.

Runner was there, in the woman's apartment.

The quarry was there.

"Come on, bastard! Jump the bitch and go home!"

The driver turned a pained expression toward the

1

burly man, but said nothing. He had given up on conversation ten minutes after being introduced to the man beside him. He was young, young enough to be the burly man's son, although the thought of a blood relationship would have horrified him. He was educated, came from a good family.

The burly man came from the streets, a fighter from his first days in the schoolyard. An incorrigible, thrown into the streets at the age of twelve, barely able to read and sign his own name. His face was coarse with his years, lined with the broken blood vessels of the constant drinker. The bulbous nose was clown red.

The driver sighed, squirming a fold of fine Irish worsted from beneath his thigh, and settled back in his seat. His overcoat cost more than the burly man's entire wardrobe. In the gray light of the night and the storm, his shadowed face seemed finely chiseled, although too cold to be really handsome. The only thing cheap about him was the pull-on rubbers protecting his ninety dollar Italian shoes, picked up early that afternoon in Boston, a hundred miles away.

"Shit! Dammit, I want a cigarette!"

The burly man tossed the lighter onto the dash and jammed his left hand deep into the pocket of his J. C. Penney all-weather coat. Despite the fake fur zip-in lining, the coat did nothing to keep the cold from his bones. Maybe Madge was right, he should start wearing long johns in cold weather. He had resisted the suggestion for years, remembering his alcoholic father. The drunken old bum wore long underwear winter and summer. For his son to give in to it now was a sign of defeat.

Dammit, he wasn't old!

In his pocket, his fingers caressed the shape of the closed knife. The gloves were expensive, fingertips as supple as a second skin despite the real fur lining across the palms. The tip of his tongue pushed against his bottom lip, forcing a gap, as he turned the familiar hardness in his fingers. An unconscious smile shaped his mouth as he dug his sharp thumbnail into the crescent indentation and worked the blade half open.

The wind gusted, stripping dead leaves from the gaunt branches of the century-old elms lining the street. The sudden blast rocked the car on its springs. The rain came down harder than ever for a period of four minutes, isolating the two men in the car. It was impossible to see the shape of the car parked just in front of them, much less the target house.

The driver ripped a paper towel from the roll beside him and began to wipe fog from the windshield, when the burly man growled a question. In response, he pushed back his sleeve and checked the illuminated crystal digits of his watch. "One-fifteen," he said.

"Shit! He's gonna stay all goddamn night."

"He has a class at eight o'clock. According to his dossier, Runner never stays all night with the woman when he has an early class the next day."

"Dossy-shit! Stop with the fancy talk, punk. All I want is to know where the target's gonna be and who's gonna be with—I think he's comin'."

The house had been converted to apartments. The door opened and a man came out, shrugging his collar around his neck. He was tall, and the porch light overhead painted his bare head orange.

"That's 'Runner, yeah. What are you waitin' for, bastard? Come on, run for it!"

The man might have heard; suddenly he dashed down the steps, water splashing wide from the sidewalk when his feet landed, and ran for the Mercedes sports car at the curb. The interior lights winked on, off. From their angle, the men across the street couldn't see the wipers start, but taillights came on; then the headlights cut twin cones through the falling rain. The car moved away from the curb and swung right, around the corner.

The driver's sleeve was worked back again, thumb and forefinger holding his glove off the watch dial. He watched the digits change, conscious of the burly man's breathing even above the pounding of his heart.

"Five minutes."

"Give it five more."

The wait continued until he marked the moment, then the burly man rolled out of the car before the driver had a chance to look up. The car remained dark; the bulb had been removed from the dome light as soon as the punk who stole it in Newton turned it over to them. He followed the other, running awkwardly, cold water splashing into his pants legs and wetting his silk socks.

The burly man waited for him on the porch, water dripping from his coat. There was nothing else to mark his sudden hundred-yard dash. He grinned as the younger man sucked in air, and turned to the door.

It was unlocked; the vestibule was just deep enough for a half-moon, marble-top table and five mailboxes. The inner door had a glass window; the hall within, obscured by lace curtains, was dimly lit by a twenty-five watt bulb in a wall sconce.

The burly man popped the lock on the inner door and they were in, brushing past the Boston fern at the foot of the stairs. He paused to listen, although the landlady was stone deaf. Then he went up the stairs, counting risers and stepping over the fifth and the eleventh.

There were four doors off the second floor landing, but only two were marked with scrolled brass letters. The driver moved to A, at the front, and knocked. The noise of the storm outside was like the distant roar of a waterfall, constant yet unheard.

The woman was there, voice muffled by the door. "Is that you, James?"

"No, Miss Blake." He spoke softly, his voice a high, feminine tenor. The burly man smirked. "I'm Agent John Kramer, Defense Intelligence Agency. We're sorry to bother you at this hour, we tried to call you, but apparently the storm knocked out the phone lines."

The chain rattled in its slot; the night latch clicked out of the way. The door cracked to the length of the chain, the four inches allowed enough to show the woman's face. She was smeared with cold cream. She peered through the crack, nearsighted eyes watering with strain.

"What is it? Let me see your identification."

The man who called himself Kramer produced a leather case and flipped it open to show the gold badge and the lucite-encased card with a bad photo. He held it close enough for her to puzzle out the name. Satisfied, she closed the door, chain rattling, and opened it all the way.

"Come in. Please excuse the way I look, I was just going to take a bath.

She wore a quilted blue robe and buff scuffs. She was blonde and still pretty, at thirty, despite the cold cream across her face.

"What is this all about?"

The burly man moved quickly through the room, which was filled with overstuffed furniture, and flattened himself against the wall by the bedroom door. A hand fumbled through the opening, hit the wall switch. He moved in quickly, belying his bulk and his age.

"Am I suspected of harboring a fugitive?" She laughed. "All he'll find is dust under the bed."

Kramer managed a small smile, but his eyes flicked from the overflowing bookcase to the television in the corner to a silver-framed photo of Sandra Blake and a man, taken ten years ago. The family resemblance was marked.

"It's about your brother, Miss Blake," he said, as the burly man searched the bedroom and then the bath. "How long has it been since you last heard from him?"

"Sam?" She shrugged, and her eyes touched a photo of the same man in uniform. "Months, I suppose—not since the Fourth of July. That's the last time we talked, on the telephone. There have been letters, of course, and we always get together on Christmas."

"Recent letters?"

"Within the month. Why?"

"Your brother seems to have disappeared."

She managed a laugh. "You think something's happened to Sam?" She shook her head, and again glanced at the photograph. "Sam's all right. If something was wrong, I'd know. We're twins, you know. If something bad happens to either of us, the other knows instantly."

The driver raised an eyebrow, and Sandra Blake colored.

"Go ahead, laugh. It's the truth."

"May we see the last few letters, Miss Blake?"

"Why not?" She shrugged. "Sam never tells me any national secrets, I can assure you. Sometimes I wish he would."

She turned away to a small Regency desk on spindly legs and pulled down the front, reaching into a cubbyhole that held a thin sheaf of letters. Kramer moved behind her and yanked the robe down from her shoulders. She gasped in protest and started to turn, but before she could scream his hand clapped across her mouth.

The woman struggled, tried to kick back at him, but the driver, whose name wasn't John Kramer, was too strong for her. He forced her arm behind her back, smothering her muffled protests.

"Hold still, damn you!"

Sandra Blake ignored his foolish command, face turning red as she fought. The burly man brought the knife from his pocket, thumbnail flicking the blade open; a snap of the wrist finished the job. The steel gleamed as the blade angled, reflecting the soft glow of electricity.

Her robe was open to the waist; he ripped it the rest of the way, revealing her nakedness. Even as she struggled, the driver forcing her captured hand painfully higher, she locked her ankles together, tried to clamp her thighs.

The burly man caught her other hand and bent the fingers back as he slid the point of his blade into the center of her pubic fur.

Spittle and mucous coated the driver's glove as Sandra Blake twisted violently against him. He yanked at her jaw nearly breaking it, as the knife sliced upward before the blood could spill. The muscle at the top of the vagina severed cleanly and blood and urine rushed out, mixed together.

The burly man stepped nimbly aside, pulling the angled blade through two inches of fatty tissue and blood vessels, revealing gray intestine as the gash opened. He grunted with the effort as the great cut split the side of the belly button, umbilical end bobbing away. The knife rose back toward the surface, broke through the skin where the heavy breasts curved together.

Breathing rapidly, the man stepped back and wiped his mouth, then reversed the knife. Her eyes glazed as he carved X's into the top of each breast. The he swung the knife with his full strength at her throat. The point came out on the other side, and he yanked it around, severing carotid and jugglar and windpipe.

Sandra Blake was dead before he finished.

The driver's face contorted as he released the body; it fell with a soft noise into the puddle of gore and piss as he ran for the bathroom. The burly man waited out the sounds of retching, turning the woman over with the tip of his rubber, careful to avoid the blood. Then he picked up the photo of brother and sister together, held it for a moment, let it fall facedown across the open wound.

The driver came out, wiping his face with a cool washcloth. His pallor was green and he looked away from the body, eyes closed.

"They wanted it rough," said the burly man. "Did you clean up in there? Wipe the toilet and flush the stuff down."

The driver was busy for nearly five minutes, his walk

still unsteady when he came out. The burly man had satisfied himself that none of the other tenants heard the low sounds of the struggle.

"At least you puked in the bowl," he said. It was the first hint of a compliment during the past twelve hours. "Let's get out of here."

They eased the door gently shut until the latch clicked, moved silently down the stairs, stepping over the squeaky risers. The burly man checked the street before stepping out onto the porch; the other houses had been dark for hours. Apparently there were no late TV fans on this street.

It was still raining. The driver had left the keys in the ignition; the motor caught at once and the wipers beat off the sheets of sliding water. One dead leaf hung on for more than a block. He didn't turn on the headlights until they were two blocks away.

TWO

The twelve Americans and the ARVN captain
moved in single file along the forest trail. Shirtless
bodies glistened as though oiled. Less than two hours
into the sky, the sun was merciless. Tongues were
thick, lips dry and cracking and tasting of salt. Some of
the teenaged soldiers thought wearily of the dubious
comforts of Base or the greater comforts of Saigon: of
hookers and mind-blasting drunks, of grass, of coke, of
the blessed joy of smack.

The big-assed bird colonel was in the lead, the
lieutenant right behind him, Sergeant Kowalski bringing up the rear. Troubleshooter, they said, when word
came down the colonel was coming to C-company.
Looking for fuckups. C-company was the right place to
look. They were young, Kowalski the oldest of the
enlisted men at twenty. Just twenty. Three of the boys
were barely eighteen. The lieutenant, twenty-two.

The ARVN captain looked no more than fourteen.
Spit and polish just like his hero, the colonel. The bird
wore his green beret cocked at the exact regulation

angle, his M-16 shining where it should, his jungle
fatigues starched and creased, his brass and his jump
boots gleaming. Hero.

Hah!

The lieutenant heard someone hack and shot a warning glare over his shoulder. Lieutenant Forbes was
human; he smoked grass with the guys—the fuckups.
Your asses have had *it* now. The colonel was a twenty-
year man, though he didn't look much older than the
lieutenant. Started in Korea, a boy wonder, got more
medals than sense. A real Hollywood-hero type asshole.

M-16's on the alert, more than one safety off against
regulations, hating the army and hating their local draft
boards and hating Lyndon Fuckass Johnson for sending
them here, most of all hating themselves for being too
stupid to figure a way out of this fucking mess, this
toilet called Vietnam, the patrol watched the forest,
conscious of its exposed position. Some, one or two of
the more imaginative, wondered what it would be like
when the fragmentation grenades and the Bouncing
Bennings went off at crotch height, making mincemeat
out of their young genitals.

The Gooks timed it right. There must have been
thirty or forty of them: the ambush worked just like the
textbooks said it should. From ground positions and
from the trees they opened with automatic rifle fire as
soon as Kowalski came into the meadow. Half of the
young Americans were dead before they could fall,
sitting ducks.

Only the big-assed colonel got away, sixth sense that
had saved him countless times dropping Runner two
seconds before the shooting started. Serial number

105-52-9722, pride of the Special Forces and the whole goddamn United States Army, but most especially the fair-haired boy of the High Command, Colonel James Curtiss Runner squirmed along on his belly, heading by instinct for the one gap in the Gook encirclement. While thirty or forty Vietcong moved in to finish wasting the patrol, Colonel Runner got away without so much as a splinter in his ass or a crease in his green beret . . .

* * *

Runner sat up in bed, the echo of a scream fading. His throat was hoarse.

He shivered, blinked several times until his eyes focused. Sweat poured off his body. A chill draft came from the window, still moisture-streaked by the steady rain. Every minute of the patrol was vivid in his memory. His fingers dug into the single blanket that served as his only covering winter and summer and clenched the fabric, his knuckles white with tension.

The sound that woke him from the nightmare started again: a sledgehammer slamming repeatedly against the door of the apartment, rattling the dishes in the kitchenette. The vibration echoed through the dry framing of the aging building, jarring crumbs of Aristex loose from the ceiling. Except for Runner's additions in the way of floor-to-ceiling bookshelves, the Aristex was the only recent rehabilitation done to the apartment.

The apartment was small but functional. The carpets came with the place, but the furniture was his, bought all at once at the nearest branch of a national discount chain. Not the cheapest, not the most expensive; like the apartment itself, the furniture served the purposes Runner demanded of it. The only article with history was the heavy mahogony desk in the alcove off the living room; it had belonged to Runner's grandfather.

The building was solid, insulating its tenants from unnecessary noise and the outside world. The tenant below Runner was in her nineties and stone deaf. The man upstairs, a bachelor in his sixties, only ran the water in the bathtub on Saturday night. Quiet.

He glanced at the clock on the nightstand: 6:47.

Morning, although still dark. Just enough light filtered through the rain to let him see major obstacles in the ruler-straight paths he had laid out. Storm clouds were as thick as ever above the roofs of the houses backing the apartments. It had been raining eighteen hours straight.

Runner yawned, cracking his jaw. In thirteen minutes the automatic alarm in his subconscious would have brought him out of the nightmare. The dream was bad, one of the worst. And thirteen minutes was enough for the dreaming mind to relive horror a hundred times, in this instance starting with the moment he had picked Lieutenant Forbes out of the mess tent and told him to order up a patrol.

The hammering started again, demanding. Wide awake, Runner swung out of the bed and stood in the draft: a solidly built man three inches over six feet. A puddle had gathered on the sill, but a slanted metal shield saved the carpet from a wetting.

If he hadn't taken the patrol out that morning, some of those kids would be alive.

The nightmare faded, sank into the less pleasant files

13

of memory. Runner's back and thighs were wrinkle-marked where he had twisted in the bedding. He wore only undershorts. The draft chilled his body.

He grabbed yesterday's gray flannels from the back of a chair and pulled them on, then circled the bed to grab a towel from the bathroom rack. Runner was dark complected, skin almost olive. Eyes so dark in color they seemed black flashed beneath lashes bleached so pale they seemed white. The improbable contrast was the result of continuing war between his Nordic and his Slav genes.

He snapped on a floor lamp and zipped up, combing his fingers through his hair. It was still the same pale shade, although forty was behind him. There were age lines not in his face back in Nam, and a two-inch long, scimitar-shaped scar curved across his left temple. Only his beard was a much darker blond, stubbling his chin and his cheeks.

He opened the door. "Yes?"

James Runner showed neither surprise nor annoyance at the two men standing in the hallway. The older was pushing sixty; he seemed embarrassed by the early hour. The younger man seemed vaguely familiar. He had a ham fist raised to knock again.

"Dr. James Runner?"

The older one asked the question. Runner shook his head.

"I'm not a doctor. I don't practice medicine."

Sixty sighed; he was big, almost bigger than Runner, although flesh sagged on his bones. He rephrased the question, eyelids drooping.

"You are James Runner?"

"Who are you?"

Identification cases came from their pockets. The older one's gold-enameled badge had Detective-Lieutenant lettered hin red. His name, according to the card on the other flap, was Cassell. He was florid-featured, jowled by age, probably reddened by alcohol. He should have been gnawing a well-chewed cigar.

The other badge was lettered in plain black and said Detective Second Grade. Ham fist was perhaps thirty, barrel-shaped and muscle-bound. His name was Mabry; his hatless hair was cropped close in a brushcut. He studied the musculature of Runner's naked torso, rising and falling on the balls of his feet as his fingers worked against each other.

Runner glanced from ID to face; the uncomplimentary photos did neither an injustice.

"You are James Runner?" asked the lieutenant again.

"I am."

"May we come in?"

"Why?"

The question surprised Cassell; he had expected a more reasonable attitude from someone of Runner's generation. It was bad enough taking guff from smart-ass punks, but, dammit, there was a limit.

Mabry's eyes gleamed. He bounced. He didn't like Runner.

"For you, War Hero," said Mabry, "we got some questions!"

"Shut up, Otto." Cassell had been up all night. He was very tired. "I think it would be better if we came in, Doctor . . . *Mr*. Runner."

The students call me professor."

"Professor." He nodded. "Please?"

Runner shrugged and stepped aside. Mabry followed the lieutenant into the apartment, disappointed. He glanced around, expression shifting subtly to a sneer at the thousands of books.

Cassell drifted through the room, glanced into the alcove. The desk was covered with working papers and opened volumes: Ephemerides for a dozen years, Lang's *Comparative Astrology, Encyclopaedia of Occultism,* both the Occidental and the Oriental volumes of *The Masks of the Gods.* Many of the volumes were old; all showed signs of much handling and use. On a short shelf above the desk was a brass astrolabe enameled in blue; he snapped on the desk lamp to look at it more closely.

"Nice," he said. "Antique?"

"Sixteenth century."

"Um. You into astrology, professor?"

"I have studied it."

"My wife bugs me every morning with my horoscope. It seems like nonsense to me."

"Astrology was the first science," said Runner. "Unfortunately, it suffers from charlatans and fools. The person who studies the field can learn."

Cassell turned away from the desk and pulled *The Magic of Mysticism* from a comfortable chair, then sat. He pulled a battered small notebook from his pocket while Runner cleared books and made space for himself on the sofa. Mabry remained standing. The lieutenant flipped through dog-eared pages, smothering a yawn.

"Do you know a Miss Sandra Blake, professor?"

Runner crossed his legs, straightening the crease in his trousers. "I know Sandra Blake, yes."

"In fact, you're close friends?"

"Close enough."

"Um." Cassell nodded approval at the verification. "I understand you and Miss Blake have been keeping company for the past six months or so."

The phrase was pompous, old-fashioned; it sounded like something the lieutenant's parents might have said when he was a small boy. Runner's mouth twitched, but his face remained blank.

"Get to the point, lieutenant. You obviously know Sandy and I have been dating. We've made no secret of our relationship, and I know of no laws we've broken. We're both of age."

Mabry grinned, a dirty smile that revealed a gold tooth on one side, a missing incisor on the other. Neither improved his looks. Cassell glanced at him, frowning, and ran the tip of his tongue between his own teeth, which were too white and even to be anything but the work of a dental technician.

"Did you see Miss Blake last night, professor?"

"Yes."

"Where did you go?"

"We had dinner, saw a movie, came home. Where did you go on your last date?"

The lieutenant colored, swallowed. Mabry bounced.

"You went with Miss Blake to her apartment?" asked Cassell. "In fact, you stayed quite late?"

"You know my movements better than I do."

"You did stay quite late?" he insisted.

"Late enough."

"Later than usual."

Runner conceded the point and the notebook closed. "What time did you leave Miss Blake's apartment, professor?"

"If it matters, lieutenant, one-fifteen. Less than six hours ago," he added, pointedly.

"Exactly one-fifteen? Not earlier, or later? Even by a few minutes?"

"Exactly one-fifteen. I waited for the rain to let up. It didn't, so I left. In case you hadn't noticed, it's still raining."

Mabry sucked in breath, worked his shoulders back a time or two, bounced again. His thumbs rubbed continuously against his forefingers.

"Do you mind telling us just where you had dinner last night, professor?"

Runner waited several seconds before answering, locking eyes with the lieutenant. Cassell blinked, but his gaze didn't waver.

"What are you investigating, lieutenant?"

Cassell consulted the notebook again, reading: "At one-fifteen this morning, professor, according to the testimony of Miss Angela Gray, a female Caucasian about fifty years of age who resides at 217 Fair Oaks Drive, Apartment B, this city, she was in her living room getting ready to close up the apartment for the night."

"I know Angela Gray," said Runner.

"Is there any reason Miss Gray should hold animosity toward you, professor?"

"None that I know of. We've spoken briefly, the few times we've met."

"Um. According to Miss Gray's testimony, she always goes to bed at that time, after watching Johnny Carson then fixing herself a cup of hot chocolate."

Runner said nothing. Cassell continued. "At one-fifteen this morning she heard Miss Blake's door open, and a brief conversation ensued between Miss Blake and a man. She recognized Miss Blake's voice, even though the door was closed. She thought she recognized your voice, professor.''

"She did. It was me.''

"Miss Gray further stated, 'Sandy sounded awful mad. They must have had an awful fight.' '' The notebook closed again. "Did you and Miss Blake argue last night, professor? This morning?'' he amended.

Runner's jaw set; his expression was suddenly colder. "That is between Miss Blake and myself.''

"Um.'' The notebook again. "Mis Gray states that she is a light sleeper. She has a Pomeranian bitch, eleven years old. The dog also is a light sleeper. At two-fifteen this morning, the dog's whining woke Miss Gray.''

Notebook closed. Runner stared, waiting.

"At first Miss Gray tried to quiet the dog, which seemed quite agitated. At last she got up and followed it to the apartment door, where it scratched until Miss Gray let it out. It immediately ran to Miss Blake's door and began scratching again, and whining. Miss Gray knocked, trying to rouse Miss Blake, without success. At last she returned to her own apartment and obtained a key she had to Miss Blake's apartment.'' Again a pause. "Did you know Miss Gray had a key to Miss Blake's apartment, professor?''

"Sandy had a cat that died last winter. She and Angela fed each other's pets when one of them was away overnight.''

"That tallies with Miss Gray's explanation. She returned with the key and let herself in to Miss Blake's apartment. The chain was off its slide.''

Runner's face could have been carved from flesh-colored ice as he waited for the lieutenant to continue, but Cassell decided to wait him out. At last he surrendered and asked the question.

"Obviously something was wrong, lieutenant. Is Sandy all right?"

Mabry exploded, taking a step closer to Runner. "You know, you filthy murderin' pervert!" His fists clenched. "God! I seen some loonies in my time, but what you did to that poor woman made me puke!"

"Otto!" Cassell's voice thundered. He seemed to straighten to his full height, although he remained seated. Mabry glared at Runner, but subsided, and the lieutenant let his own eyes move back to him, blinking.

"Mis Blake was dead."

"You think I killed her." It wasn't a question.

Mabry threw up his hands. "Jesus! Look at the heartless son of a bitch, Andy! Cut her up like guttin' out a fish and doesn't turn a hair on his perverted head!"

"Shut up, Otto! One more time and I'll send you down to the car, have Browning up here."

Cassell levered himself out of his chair, glowering at Mabry, and pulled a folded legal form from his pocket. He tapped the paper against his palm several times, then sighed and brought out a much-handled three by five index card.

"Professor Runner, did you or do you now have any knowledge of the circumstances concerning or leading to Miss Blake's death?"

Runner's jaw was set. "None."

"Did you and Miss Blake argue last evening?"

"That is immaterial, since our discussions had nothing to do with . . . what happened."

"Very well." He glanced at the card. "Professor James Runner, I have here a warrant for your arrest on a charge of suspicion of murder in the first degree. You have the right to remain silent. You have the right to have a lawyer at your side while being interrogated. If you cannot afford a lawyer, one will be appointed for you by the court. If you choose to waive any of your rights, anything you say may be held against you in a court of law."

He lowered the card. "Do you choose to waive any of your rights?"

Runner stood. "I do not."

"Do you have a lawyer you wish to call?"

"I can get one. Am I allowed to make the call here?"

"At the station house. Please get dressed."

Cassell and Mabry followed him into the bedroom, crowding into the narrow space along the wall while he stripped off flannels and shorts, brought fresh underwear from the dresser. The lieutenant looked away, studying the books on the nightstand. His face was impassive, his lids once again lowered sleepily. Mabry's eyes never left Runner. He was bouncing again, seemed ready to explode.

Runner dressed quickly in sports shirt and sweater, transferring keys, change and wallet to the new trousers. Then he returned to the living room to take a lined jacket from the front closet. While he slipped it on Mabry brought out handcuffs.

Cassell paused in the bedroom door, looked longingly toward the bathroom. He seemed suddenly embarrassed again.

"Excuse me, but I hope you don't mind if I use your bath, professor. It's been a long night."

Runner smiled. "Be my guest."

Scowling, Mabry waited for the lieutenant to duck around the corner before snapping the cuffs on Runner's wrists. He squeezed them as tight as he could, forcing the jaws into the flesh. Runner started to protest, and Mabry smiled, twisting them.

"Come on, War Hero! Try something! Please!"

Runner stared into his eyes. "Do I know you?"

"No, but I know you," he answered, speaking low. "I was in Nam when you took that bunch of kids out to get their heads blown off."

Runner shifted his weight. "Is that supposed to mean something?"

"One of them boys was the kid brother of a good buddy of mine. A guy in my company."

"I'm sorry."

"Nah, asshole! Sorry ain't enough. He wanted to kill you, you ball-bustin' brass hero! He wanted to watch you die slow. He prayed you'n he'd get grabbed by the Gooks and thrown into the same prison camp. A murderin' maniac, that's what he called you, but you got away with it. This time I'm here to promise you you won't get away!"

The sucker punch caught Runner in the stomach as water roared in the bathroom. He doubled over, grunting, but Mabry grabbed him by the shoulders and forced him straight.

"Just a sample, bastard! There'll be more!"

Cassell came back, saw the strain in Runner's expression. The lieutenant looked quickly to Mabry, but the detective was opening the door. Runner moved into the hall before Mabry could grab his arm.

A cruiser waited at the curb, its blue light turning idly while the cold rain drizzled down from leaden skies. Despite the hour, a dozen people had gathered on the sidewalk, umbrellas raised. As the two policemen led Runner out of the building a man jumped from another car and took a series of flash pictures, blinding those not quick enough to close their eyes.

The back seat of the car was a cage. Mabry opened the rear door, gave Runner just enough shove to make him stumble. He banged his knee and his shoulder, and that gave Mabry one more chance to twist the cuffs. Then the detective climbed in beside him while the lieutenant took the front seat, next to the uniformed driver.

The car's wipers worked noisily, smearing the windshield as the cruiser moved away from the curb, leaving the idly curious to turn around and stare at the apartment building. Runner gazed through the wire-screened window conscious of the closed-in feeling—first taste of jail coming. The tight cuffs slowed, nearly stopped circulation in his hands, which quickly became numb and chilled. But the discomfort meant nothing.

He had let Sandy start another of her meaningless arguments, born like most out of post-coital let down. This time she called him a robot, a man without a soul. He said he counted the strokes while they made love. He left her in her black mood, knowing she would be the one to call and make up in the morning.

But Sandy was dead.

The evidence must be strong against him, or the court would not have so quickly issued a warrant. Somebody had killed Sandy . . .

And the killer was trying to set him up for it.

THREE

The police station was three rooms in a corner of the county courthouse basement: a cubbyhole for the chief; a larger duty room that had once been two storerooms, shared now by Cassell, Mabry and another detective, who together investigated all matters needing criminal investigation; and the public area, a battered oak desk behind a waist-high fence and three woden benches. Behind the desk a closet had been converted into a radio room. The unattanded radio made static to itself when Runner arrived.

The courthouse had been built in 1914 to serve the needs of the rural county and the village's then three thousand. At that time the university was a private denominational college a mile west of the town line with one hundred twenty students. The college was successful; the town was not. The campus spread east, the town grew not at all until Kraft built a full-time cheese factory in the mid-fifties. That stirred a minor industrial boom. Now AMF had a bowling pin factory and there were several small electronics plants taking advantage of the clean air. In the last twenty years the population of the town doubled, while the university exploded out of its campus.

University populations tend to be activist; small towns tend to be snobbish. Until the late sixties the two groups tolerated each other. Now there was a student and an assistant professor on the Board of Selectmen, opposed by three villagers who claimed roots to the eighteenth century. One of these years the balance would swing the other way.

There was no crowd outside the courthouse when the cruiser pulled up in front of the ivy-covered red brick building with its Corinthian columns that needed painting, but a man with a minicam popped out of the building as Runner was half-yanked out of the car by Mabry. There was no reporter; the cameraman worked for the station in the city, and was allowed to bring the camera home with him at night. Usually it paid off with fires or gory accidents. This was the first murder in the town limits within memory.

Cassell shunted the cameraman away as he led the small procession into the basement. Behind the desk, an overaged sergeant, belly straining the lower buttons on his shirt, sat listening wearily to the phone. He hung up, relieved, while Mabry removed the cuffs at Cassell's order. The lieutenant slumped on the edge of the desk while Mabry went to a coffee maker and a uniformed patrolman appeared to take Runner's photograph and fingerprints. The camera seemed older than the building. The patrolman was young and talkative.

"Ever have your prints taken?"

"Yes." Runner didn't elaborate.

"In the service, I bet—" He spotted the cuff marks on Runner's wrists. "Lieutenant!"

Cassell sighed and came over to eye the bruises. The skin was broken on both wrists.

"Shit!"

He turned; Mabry faced the other direction, leaning on a file cabinet. He didn't hear Cassell's approach. The lieutenant's heavy brogan shot out and caught him square in the meat of the ass. Mabry went flying, cup spraying coffee, and caught himself just short of crashing into the wall.

"What the fuck—"

"Shut up! You stupid asshole!" Cassell trembled with anger. "I warned you, fuckhead! This time I write you up!"

He stalked from the room without giving Mabry a chance to reply. The detective glared hatred at Runner and went out into the basement. The patrolman gave Runner a paper towel to wipe his fingers.

The sergeant had finished inventorying the items in his pockets, glared as he gave Runner the list for his signature. He snatched the paper back quickly.

"Let him use the phone in the chief's office, Cox."

The patrolman led the way, pulled the phone to the front of another battered desk, then leaned against the doorframe. A moment later there was an uproar outside, and Chief Forey came in. He eyed Runner with distrust. Forey was in his fifties, grizzled and white-haired, the outdoors type. Wearing rumpled khakis, he fell into his squeaking chair.

The phone barked a surly growl into Runner's ear. During the trip downtown he had considered his choices in contacts, deciding on his department head, even though Dr. Howard never liked him. Now he explained the situation to the incredulous Howard.

"You want the university to send a lawyer?"

"As soon as possible, yes."

"He'll have to come up from the city. Why not a local man? Keith Devlin's okay."

"Anyone you recommend, doctor. And you better find someone to cover my classes and lectures. I don't know how long it will take these people to come to their senses."

Howard growled agreement, then added, "I won't ask if you did it, Runner. If you did, you'd lie."

"I didn't." He cradled the buzzing phone and looked at the chief who had gone out and come back with coffee. "What's the procedure now?"

Forey seemed embarrassed. Runner had met him at a time or two at university social functions.

"Did you do it?"

"No."

"Wish I knew how good a liar you are. Once you're arraigned, if the judge refuses bail, you'll be sent to the city. They take our prisoners if the sentence is more than thirty days. Now you'll be in one of our cells."

The jail was across the basement, twelve cells in facing rows. Each was furnished with two army cots bolted to the floor, a seatless toilet and a sink with running water.

Cox led the way, placing Runner in the last inside cell. Those across the way had casement windows set twelve inches below the sidewalk. At the moment the windows were covered halfway or more with dirt and dead leaves. Two of the cells had water trickling down the wall, turning the institutional green to rust.

Runner shared the block with two old drunks and a badly beaten youth. The boy sat listlessly on the edge of his cot, glancing up when Runner passed. One eye was closed, the other puffy, while his lip swelled enormously on one side. His right hand was bandaged.

"The loser?"

"The winner," said Cox. "He also started it."

"Is this the best you have?" Runner asked, staring into the cell.

"Sorry," said Cox. "This is the honeymoon suite."

"I won't marry here. Any chance of breakfast?"

"I'm afraid not, professor. Breakfast is at six. Lunch at 11:30 and supper at four. If you want, you can order from the diner. In fact, I'd advise it."

"You took my money."

"When the check comes you can sign an authorization slip."

"I'll remember that."

Cox closed the barred door and moved out of sight; then came a thunderous crash as the locking bar dropped into place. Apparently they hadn't bothered locking in the drunks and the fighter.

The partitions between the cells were solid; he could no longer smell the old man who had soiled himself. The stink was replaced by the deeper, more lasting acrid smell of ammonia used as disenfectant.

Runner scanned the visible corridor and then his eyes fell to the chipped paint of his bars. Neither was interesting. He turned, studied his cell for twenty seconds, imprinting its details in his memory. He sat on one of the cots. The springs creaked noisily and the thin mattress was rock hard. But the bedding was clean, though threadbare. The pillow proved harder than the mattress.

He tossed the pillow onto the other cot and bent to pull off his shoes. He had chosen them because there were no laces for his jailers to remove. They had taken his belt. He stretched out on the cot. Five hours of sleep was usually enough, but twenty years in the army taught Runner to take advantage of the moment. He regulated his breathing and let a forearm fall across his eyes to shield them from the naked bulb in the overhead; the bulb was protected by a heavy wire cage. He slept.

*   *   *

"Professor Runner?"

Runner had turned on his side. His eyes opened as the locking bar crashed out of its sockets, and he came to his feet.

"I'm Keith Devlin."

The lawyer was graying, stocky, a foot shorter than Runner. A massive moustache curved back to become part of untamed sideburns. He swung the door open and held out his hand as Cox appeared.

"Mr. Devlin." Runner shook hands. "What time is it?"

"Just after nine. Sorry I couldn't get here sooner, but my wife's car broke down. I had to take her to work, out to the university. The book store. Perhaps you know her?"

"Not by name. Sorry."

"Oh, well. We can talk in the duty room. It will be more comfortable."

Cassell and Mabry were gone; the duty room was empty. Devlin sat at a library table, across from Runner, offering a cigarette that was refused.

"The, uh, murder has caused quite a commotion, bigger than anything since the students took over the dean's office ten years ago and the governor called out the National Guard. Were you here then?"

"I was in the army." A battered, tin pie plate served as ashtray; it hadn't been emptied for a long time. "Any chance this place is bugged?"

Devlin laughed. "Not in this town. The selectmen won't approve a new box of paperclips in the budget."

He opened his attache case, brought out a legal size, lined yellow tablet and three felt tip pens: one in black, one in red, one in green. Then he laced his fingers on top of the table.

"I must tell you, professor, this is out of my territory. I'm not a criminal lawyer. Oh, I defend local people who get into minor scrapes, kids who take a car and go joyriding, and the like. I can represent you at the arraignment, if the district attorney decides to proceed with a complaint, but for the trial work I suggest bringing in the experts."

"Whoever you say."

"Kornauer, Wiley are the best in the state. Of course, they are expensive . . ."

Runner shrugged. "Money is no problem."

"Well, that's good."

Devlin's eyes fell to the pad and he picked up the black pen, tapping it. At last he sighed and faced Runner again.

"Professor, did you kill Sandra Blake?"

"I did not."

"We better get the facts down." Another sigh. "You better get used to telling your story. You'll probably have to give it a hundred times before the trial."

"I've given evidence in army proceedings and court-martials, Mr. Devlin."

The little lawyer nodded, pleased. For the next twenty minutes he led Runner through the events of the previous night, and through his relationship with Sandra Blake. A dozen sheets of yellow paper filled with large scribblings, salient points marked in red and boxed in green. At last he let the pen drop.

"I think Chief Forey moved too fast on the warrant. Unless, of course, he has evidence we don't know about. The police have forty eight hours to take their complaint before the district attorney. He'll make the decision if the case is strong enough." He nibbled his lip. "I think the decision has already been made. There's political hay to be made in a case like this."

"What then?"

"You'll be arraigned. The judge will set a court date for the preliminary hearing. He has the option of whether or not to grant bail. Considering your record of service, bail should be just a formality. I'll try to move things along as quickly as possible."

Pad and pens went back into the attache case, which closed with brisk snaps of the latches. He stood.

"There are reporters outside, professor. I'd advise not talking to them. Not yet."

"I've nothing to say."

"Good. Is there anything I can get you?"

"Reading material, if I'm to be here overnight."

"I'll send over something appropriate." He offered his hand again as Runner stood. "I'm sure everything is going to work out, professor."

Cox popped in when Devlin opened the door, a science-fiction paperback closed about his thumb. He took Runner back to his cell and thirty minutes later appeared with the morning paper from the city and the ones from Boston, and a stack of magazines. The latter included the news weeklies, *Harper's*, *The Atlantic Monthly*, *Atlas*.

Runner dropped the lot onto the vacant cot and stretched out again. He had a great deal to think about.

*   *   *

A door slammed; Runner's eyes opened. Light spilled through the bars. Footsteps approached his cell. The night-shift desk sergeant saw he was awake.

"Visitor." He hacked, looked as though he wanted to spit.

"What time is it?"

"Two-thirty. In the mornin'," he added, unnecessarily.

Runner threw off the sheet and sat up; he felt grubby, could smell his own stink. The cell was overheated, much too warm. He rubbed his chin, the stubble much heavier, and tried to swallow the sour taste in his throat.

"Do you always allow visitors this late?"

"If they're government men. Get dressed."

Runner pulled on the same clothes he had worn yesterday. Devlin had returned late in the afternoon, but there was no particular news. The arraignment wasn't to be held until the allowed time had elapsed.

A young boy, no more than sixteen, sat up when the bar crashed. He had come in during the day. There were still two old drunks, although Runner couldn't have said whether it was the same two or not. One groaned at the noise; the other didn't stir.

"What government man?" he asked as the sergeant led him back to the duty room.

"He said not to tell you."

The door was open. Runner stared at the thickset man who sat on the edge of a desk, facing away. Red hair burned bright across his head except for a bald spot the size of a clenched fist. He seemed familiar; he turned.

Runner's voice was flat. "Monaghan."

"Ah, Jamie me boy!"

The greeting boomed, the voice jovial. Freckles spilled across Monaghan's forehead and slipped down to his cheekbones. His nose was peeling from sunburn.

"You can leave us now, sergeant, that's a darlin'."

"Gotta cover the desk," said the sergeant, affable now. "Holler if you want something."

"We'll do that very thing, thank you."

Monaghan sat on the edge of the desk again, leg swinging idly. He produced cigarettes, didn't offer them; he made a show of lighting one.

"Still the phony brogue." Runner stifled a yawn and dropped into one of the chairs at the table.

"To tell the truth, Jamie, I've been talkin' this way so long it's the only way I know."

Monaghan smiled. "I'd heard you buried yourself in some jerkwater university, Jamie. But why in the name of God did you come here?"

"They offered a job I wanted."

"Teachin' Oriental philosophy and Eastern religions?" He clucked his tongue and shook his head. "Those who knew you and loved you made allowances for your peculiarities, Jamie, but to come to this!"

"I like what I do, Monaghan. Can you say the same?"

"Ah, an' indeed I can, Jamie. There're those of your old friends who think it not natural that a man of your talents should waste himself this way. God-given talents, Jamie. You were one of the best."

He puffed at his cigarette, holding it daintily between middle finger and thumb, waiting for Runner to reply. Runner stared, impassive.

"It's not too late, you know. You can still come back at your old rank, Jamie."

"No."

"Seven years is a long time to think, Jamie. You did say you would think on it."

"I did. I did not change my mind."

He shook his head again. "Stubborn as always."

"I resigned my commission because I could no longer stomach the double dealings of the government and the bald-faced liars who formulate military policy."

"Noble words." Monaghan nodded. "I wish we could all afford to be as noble."

"Brownnosed your way to a star yet, Monaghan?"

"Not I, Jamie." He laughed. "As a matter of fact, I pulled a Jamie Runner, got out with my twenty years. Three years ago, that was."

"Your crimes caught up with you."

"Not at all. You know I was always good at covern'

my tracks, Jamie. I was due to make bird, but there's no future in it any more. The Irish are no longer an oppressed minority, so there's no stars floatin' around for the undereducated likes of me. Now you," he said, swinging his legs again. "The bettin' at the War College said you'd be three star now. Commandant of West Point the last two years. Now wouldn't that be something to see? A brash boy joinin' the army at seventeen an' risin' to be Chairman of the Joint Chiefs!" Monaghan sighed. "We did have dreams once, Jamie."

"You had daydreams. I won't ask what you're doing now, why you're here. You're going to tell me whether or not I want to know."

Another laugh. "I took the pension, Jamie. Did you really refuse it?" Runner shrugged. "I did what any wise man in my shoes would do, moved into Civil Service. Sort of a lateral, you might say. Made the most of my limited qualifications."

"Intelligence," said Runner.

"Bright as ever, lad."

"Langley?"

"Lord love us, no! Those fellas have much too black an image for an eagle scout like me. You know me, Jamie. I come out of the south side of Chicago an' all I ever wanted was respectability."

"All you ever wanted was to die fucking at the age of ninety."

"And I'll make it yet. I'm with Defense, Jamie. The great unwashed American public doesn't know it, but right now DIA is more important than the Company."

Runner lay his hands on the table. They stared at each other: old antagionists, reluctant allies.

"What do you want, Monaghan?"

"We got us a problem, Jamie. Not just DIA, but the entire intelligence community. Some bright fella thought you might be the one to solve our problem."

"You."

"Never did anyone say Phil Monaghan denied credit when it was due. What do you say?"

"No. I won't be co-opted."

"This time it's in your best interest, Jamie. Times have changed. Things have changed, in Washington and around the world. I think you ought to slow down and think a bit. Think a lot."

"No." Runner stood. "Go, Monaghan. Go home and tell your brass it didn't work."

Monaghan sighed again, an exaggerated intake of breath accompanied by a slow shake of the head. "I just can't believe you when you tell me you're happy, buried a hundred miles from nowhere, Jamie. Hell, you were always a man to get out an' do, not sit an' think about it."

"I've changed."

"I guess you did." He hung his head, peered slyly from the corner of his eye. "You're in big trouble, Jamie."

"So they tell me. I didn't kill the girl."

"I believe you. Takin' out a woman was never your way. I remember times that caused us problems. But to do it so messily . . ." Again he shook his head. "You're neat, Jamie. Everything in life ordered, everything in its special place. The only messy thing about you is your books, spillin' all over the place." He paused, took in air. "Did they tell you exactly how she died, Jamie?"

"Only that she was cut badly."

Monaghan crossed to a desk, took several photographs from a file folder and held them out. Runner looked at the top, taking it in his fingers. It was in black and white, but the edges of the gaping wound were sharply defined by the strong light used by the cameraman.

"We know why she was killed Jamie."

All traces of Monaghan's brogue had vanished. Runner blinked, then shook his head, as though he hadn't heard. The photograph rested on his thigh.

"What?" Shock subsided. "What did you say?"

"We know why the girl was killed."

"Why?" He came to his feet, crumpling the photograph. Cords tightened in his neck and his shoulders rippled with tension. "Who did it?"

"The identity, identities, we don't know. Not yet. We know the motive. The who is what we're hopin' you'll find out for us."

"You're a bastard, Monaghan!"

"That I am. 'Born out of wedlock,' it says that right on my birth certificate." He cocked a finger, let his thumb-hammer fall. "But we're talkin' about you, Jamie. For us, your involvement is just a happy coincidence, but one we're gonna take full advantage of."

Runner swallowed, stomach hollow and aching. He felt a stinging at the corner of his eyes.

"Why was she killed? *Why?*"

The finger-gun flicked the top of Monaghan's nose. "You'll help us, Jamie. We know you didn't kill the girl, but if you don't help us, sure as Jesus is a Christian, we'll let you hang for her murder."

FOUR

Runner exploded into rage, his vision hazing with red as he lunged for Monaghan. The photograph fell from his hand, a crumpled ball, as he grabbed the stocky agent by the shirt front. Fabric ripped, and Monaghan flinched away as Runner's left hand rose to strike openhanded.

"Jamie!"

The cry was a distant echo in Runner's ears. The world was a tunnel before him, blood rushing through his veins a roar that deafened him to the agent's protests. He could see Monaghan's mouth working, the man's hands clawing at the death grip of Runner's hand. He saw his own veins standing out from his flesh, blue pipelines feeding his anger.

Time froze: Runner stopped breathing until his heart began to triphammer in his breast. Ten seconds passed, then twenty; Monaghan brought his hands up in a try to break Runner's hold, chopping at his wrist. He saw the blows land in slow motion, saw the flesh of his arm turn white, but felt nothing.

"Runner!"

Monaghan was choking, the pressure of his shirt collar cutting off breath. But the berserker rage ebbed, the madness leaving Runner's mind. He stared at his hand . . . suddenly let his fingers open.

The agent sagged away, gasping, just as the desk sergeant came lumbering through the door, fumbling for his gun. He started to draw the pistol, but Monaghan waved him off.

"It's all right, sergeant. All right."

The agent moved back three paces as he said it, and the sergeant eyed Runner dubiously. The latter turned to face him, hands out at his side.

"Mr. Monaghan stumbled, sergeant. I helped him up."

"That's right," the agent agreed. "If I need you, I'll give you a holler."

When the man left, he added, "That was stupid, Jamie."

"It was. I wanted to kill you."

Monaghan forced a laugh as he straightened his tie; the shirt was rent beneath it. He fumbled another cigarette from the pack. It took half a dozen strikes on the lighter before he could draw smoke. He coughed and brushed the back of his hand across his mouth.

"You couldn't kill me, Jamie. Not you. Never the noble Colonel Runner. There were times I wanted to kill you, ten years ago, but you were the pope. That's what everyone in Nam called you, you know. The pope, the high priest, the grand lama."

"They had other names for you," said Runner.

"No doubt." Monaghan shrugged. "Once I almost

did kill you, you know. Almost found the nerve. I had the grenade ready to throw into your room, but I chickened out. Sometimes I wonder if I should hate myself for not killing you.''

The revelation was surprising; then Runner remembered the years of jealousy on the part of the younger man. Their careers collided in Nam and ever after they were antagonists. Runner was aware of infighting and backbiting, but he ignored it. In those days his only thought was of doing his job to perfection. His superiors decided he was a leader, and so he led. Later they used him as a troubleshooter, and so he went in to trouble spots and cleaned out the problems. Some careers were destroyed because of his efficiency, and some men, equally officers and enlisted men, were kicked out with bad conduct or dishonorable discharges. A few were sent to Leavenworth.

Runner the robot. Maybe they were right, then. Maybe he was always a robot. Little Jamie Runner drew attention as a child genius, accepted by a dozen universities when he was eleven. He was to be the youngest university student in the United States since the American Revolution when scarlet fever sent him to bed for six months.

It was while bedridden that Runner first became interested in astrology, and from that developed his love of Oriental philosophy. For a time he read deeply into the occult, putting it aside only when it became clear that charlatanism controlled the field.

At this time he also began a program of exercises to restore his strength. By the time he entered Princeton, just before his fourteen birthday, he was adept in weight lifting and wrestling. Only his physical immaturity kept him from competing on a weight level with his classmates.

Runner earned his bachelor of arts degree at sixteen, his first bachelor of science six months later. He transfered to Johns Hopkins, intending to follow his parents into medical research . . . but that summer something happened that forever changed his life. His parents were killed in a laboratory accident.

Friends of the Runners thought they were too busy to give their son affection, but they were wrong. Their death was severely felt by the still emotionally immature youth. Runner became a ward of his paternal grandfather. He threw over his university plans. The old man gently led him into psychoanalysis, and the analyst recommended he be allowed to join the army at seventeen.

Too young for a commission, Runner entered the infantry and was sent to Korea. His mental discipline made him a perfect soldier. He advanced quickly through the ranks, earning a Silver Star and then a battlefield commission.

After the death of his parents, Runner divorced himself from emotion. He formed no close attachments, made no real friends. He was introduced to sex in basic training, but for him it remained faceless. Even since his resignation his affairs were more a matter of convenience. Sandy was only a sexual outlet. Maybe she was right when she accused him of counting his strokes.

This rage that had come upon him was something new in Runner's experience. Perhaps it was all the years of emotional hiding trying to break free. Whatever, it made him, who had always been sure of himself, no longer the man in control.

Filled with disgust at what he had almost done, Runner sighed and closed his eyes. His head dropped back, rolled while he rotated his shoulders to ease the tension that had left him damp with cold sweat. When his eyes opened he stared a moment at the asbestos-wrapped steam pipe crossing the peeling ceiling.

He sighed again, and shook his head as he straightened, balling his fist in the small of his back. The basement office had the smell of old dank, and in the absolute silence of the moment he listened to the night sounds of the building and heard a faint skittering that might have been rats in the walls.

"Tell me what you know, Monaghan."

"Not enough, Jamie." The agent drew up a chair and reversed it, sat down with his arms crossed on top. "And first you give me your word you're with us."

"I'll listen."

"Not good enough. We want you, but we need a commitment right now."

"All right. My stake is personal. I'll help."

"Good." He breathed a sigh of relief. "Fortunately your security clearance was never lifted. Everything I tell you now is top secret, of course."

Runner stared, Monaghan lifting his chin to look up at him. At last the agent shrugged.

"Sandra Blake had a brother. A twin."

"Sam," agreed Runner.

"Have you met him?"

"No. Sandy mentioned him often."

"You know he was her only living relative?"

"Yes."

"Samuel Blake was an agent. DIA."

The revelation didn't bring the reaction Monaghan expected. When he waited for a reply, Runner shrugged.

"I knew he worked in Washington, but not his capacity."

"He was staff, but on temporary domestic assignment. An old friend from college days knew Blake was in Intelligence. He was a former radical, one of those wanted, although not very much. He'd been in hiding for six years, but said he wanted to come out."

"You keep saying 'was,' Monaghan."

"Sam Blake is dead."

Again Runner failed to react. Monaghan hid disappointment as the other waited impassively for him to continue.

"The contact had information of interest to several of the agencies. He set the meet for San Francisco— Berkeley, actually. Blake was to meet him at 10:45 yesterday evening in a coffee house. Day before yesterday, now. But it's still yesterday, San Francisco time."

"Blake was taken before the meet?"

"In the coffee house. He was there early, of course, and the place was covered by agents inside and out. At 10:31 PM, according to the other agents inside, Blake was sitting with two students, a boy and a girl. Apparently they didn't know him, he was just passing time until the meet. We're checking them out, of course."

He fumbled another cigarette from the pack, lit this one on the first try. He sucked the smoke deep into his lungs, let it trickle between his teeth as he continued.

"Blake was talking, something about the futility of democracy according to the girl, when he suddenly gave a strangled croak and began to thrash around violently. Both chair and table went over in his convulsions. The crowd near him panicked, and by the time any agent could reach him, he was dead."

"Poisoned?"

"No. Although the police and the medical examiner thought that at first. The witnesses said he arched his back and began to shake violently. It looked as though he was trying to pry something away from his throat, although nothing was seen. He struggled no more than twenty seconds, perhaps less, before collapsing."

"Was there an autopsy?"

"Yes, quickly, once heat was applied from Washington. It showed nothing. Blake was in excellent health, a jogger, except for a few cavities."

"There are poisons that leave no trace."

"And some kill nastily. But that's a false trail. We have other evidence to show what really happened. Consider the time element."

Runner had. "He died at 1:31 AM yesterday."

"Sandra Blake was brutally murdered at 1:31 AM."

He considered the statement. "You have proof?"

"Proof enough, with other facts we have. The local coroner does medical examinations in this county, although he's also in private practice. He reached Sandra Blake's apartment about four, and at that time set the time of death between one and two."

Runner turned over a hand, saw that it trembled. "What can I say? You want me to believe Sam Blake died from psychic trauma caused by the murder of his sister."

"They were known to be very close. Both told friends that if something bad happened to one, the other knew at the same moment."

"There are recorded instances of strong psychic attachment between close relatives," said Runner. "But I've read no reports of psychic death caused in that manner."

"In the last eighteen months, three intelligence agents serving in different agencies died in circumstances similar to Sam Blake. All three had identical twin brothers. Blake was number four, and the first in which the twin was openly murdered. The other incidents seemed to be accidents."

"They weren't."

"No. Number one's brother was an Episcopal priest and known to be depressed because of his brother's service. He drank prussic acid from his challice. It burned out his throat. His brother choked to death."

"Any evidence pointing to murder?"

"No, and we still don't have anything concrete. Only the inference from the others. There's no real evidence on number three, either."

"What about number two?"

"His brother was on a skiing trip in the Colorado Rockies when he piled his car into the side of a mountain at a hundred miles an hour. The body was recovered, but the wreckage was left in the bottom of a canyon. Six months later, after number three, a team went down and recovered the car. The brake line had been cut and the accelerator and ignition gimmicked so he couldn't shut off the motor."

"What happened to number three?"

"Burned to death in an apartment fire. A dozen old

people were killed in the same fire. We got a court order and dug up the body. He was drugged, but it could have been self-ingested.''

"You said the agents worked for different agencies. How did you tumble?''

"Pure luck. A file clerk supervisor in Social Security, a little GS-7, had all three cases pass through her hands for closing. She reads nothing but spy stories. She checked them out and took the files to her supervisor. His wife is a secretary and transcribes the meetings of the national Security Council. She took the wild story to her boss.

"Which brings us right down to you. A list was pulled of all agents with twins, and when Sam Blake died the computer went crazy. I was in New Orleans, but orders sent me running to San Francisco. While I was on the plane, one of your old friends found out you're ass deep in this thing, so I didn't even have a chance to take a leak in the airport before they had me on a plane to Boston.''

Runner breathed deeply, aware of his own stink. He rubbed his chin, his beard scratching his fingers. His sense of propriety was offended by being dirty. A man in combat couldn't take care of the niceties, but there was no excuse for not being clean in civilization.

Sandy was dead; he accepted Monaghan's fantastic explanation as motive. He knew he wanted to find the killer and repay the crime. Slowly.

"Why me, Monaghan? Why involve me?''

"We think you're just a patsy, Jamie. Someone who might have a motive. It's common knowledge your affair with the girl was less than ideal. There're several reports of Sandra Blake getting upset with you in public.'' He forced a grin. ''Knowin' you, I don't understand why you put up with her.''

''I . . . liked her.''

''Thinkin' about marriage?''

''No. Not that. Not that . . .''

Runner looked inward, examining his conscience. Why had he stayed with Sandy? The affair started as a matter of convenience, at least for him. Of sexual release. Twice a week he took Sandy to dinner, sometimes to a show, then took her home and to bed. Very convenient. No emotional attachment at all.

Or was there? Almost from the beginning Sandy gave signs the affair was going to be stormy, but Runner made no attempt to break it off. He rationalized that a woman was a woman, even though she upset his preference for calm, for peace and quiet at all times. When he first moved into the apartment he bought a television, but he couldn't remember the last time he had turned it on. Years . . .

He chose the apartment because it was quiet. Other people had stereos, at times it seemed as though the younger generation had been born with plastic growths inserted into their ears. Runner didn't even have a radio. He didn't take the daily newspapers, had divorced himself from the political process; he hadn't registered to vote.

Five years ago, even three, the affair with Sandy would have ended with the first argument. This year he had stayed. He marveled at the evolution in his own feelings.

''Were all four agents investigating the same situation?''

''Not that we knew about,'' said Monaghan. ''Not

until after number three. He was freelance, incidentally, workin' for the FBI on a Mafia matter. Now we add two and two together, and come up with twenty-two. We don't believe in coincidences, Jamie."

"What were they investigating?"

Monaghan yawned, jaw cracking. "It's been a long day, Jamie. Thirty-six hours long."

He produced another cigarette, this time coughing when the smoke went down the wrong way. Before he could continue he went to the water cooler at the far end of the duty room and drank three cups.

"There's somethin' new in the way of conspiracies, Jamie," he said, returning. "This one seems to cut across the traditional lines. We know the revolutionists are involved, and at least one black power organization. But it doesn't stop there. The Mafia is connected, and at least one religious cult. But even though we've infiltrated several of the groups, the control is someplace else. Maybe even out of the country."

"Do you know the goals?"

"Power. Maybe world domination, maybe just the USA. There's money behind them at every step. We figure Sandra Blake was taken out by hit men workin' a contract. Probably two of them: one to hold her while the other . . . Well." He didn't finish the thought. "I'll be your case officer. The computers are workin' overtime, pullin' out every detail of Sam Blake's life, and his sister's. A staff of analysts is digestin' what we have, comparin' it to the other three cases."

"Have they come up with anything?"

"Two of the first three collected coins, all three subscribed to *Time* and a couple of other magazines. When we pull it all together, maybe you can find somethin' somewhere in the movements, the contacts, of those eight people to tell us how the agents were compromised. And who did it.''

Suddenly the air went out of Monaghan's lungs; he seemed twenty years older as fatigue lines cut deep into his features. He sat down.

"I have an identical twin, Jamie.''

Runner stared. Monaghan looked down at his hands, examining his fingernails. They were grubby from the hours he had been up, although at some point he had run an electric razor across his face.

"Paul is retarded. Severely. He has no mind, there's no way you can reach him. He sits all day and stares at wherever he's lookin' when he was put down.

"My folks kept Paul home until we were six,'' he continued. ''The doctors said they had to separate us, or I'd end up the same way. We couldn't communicate, Paul and me, but just like those other people, I knew when he was hurt. When he was hungry. When he crapped his diapers I had to get to the bathroom fast or explode. Sometimes I couldn't make it when he peed. I didn't stop wetting my bed until after Paul was sent to a state institution.

"I try not to think about my brother,'' Monaghan said, his voice dropping low. ''But he's still alive. Sometimes, when things are just right, I slide right into his mind.''

He looked up. "His empty mind. When I'm inside Paul's head I see people all around me, but I can't touch them. I stare at whatever he's starin' at. Sometimes the people take me by the hand, feed me, put a clean nightshirt on me or take one off. Sometimes they roll me on a bed into the shower an' turn a hose on me so they can clean off the shit. I don't care what they do. Paul doesn't care.''

He was silent a moment, then blinked, forced a laugh. ''Ah, look at me now!'' The brogue was back. ''Bawlin' like a baby!''

Monaghan shook his head, and then turned serious again. ''I never told anyone about my brother. My twin. I haven't seen Paul since my parents took me to the state school on our fourteenth birthday. I haven't wanted to see him . . . .''

He swallowed, painfully. ''I don't want to die, Jamie. Not that way.''

FIVE

Monaghan sighed and closed his eyes, as though embarrassed by revealing his soul. For the next twenty minutes Runner questioned him closely on every detail of the four linked deaths, and on what was known about the people he thought responsible.

"The organization is young, Jamie, but it's moving fast. The first hint of something bigger in the works popped up less than three years ago. We think they're working to a timetable, but what's next on the schedule, we don't know. We want to know very much."

A few minutes later Monaghan left, promising to have Runner out as soon as pressure could be brought to bear on the local DA. Runner was left to the surly care of the sergeant, who returned him to his cell, locking him in again. This time there were curses and protests from the two youths and one of the old drunks.

"Jesus, man! Shut it off!"

The sergeant growled and left, and Runner stretched

out on the cot again. He lay awake until the sergeant returned at 5:45, turning on the lights and yelling.

"Roll out, sleeping beauties! Out!"

Breakfast arrived a few minutes later, sent over from the kitchen of the county hospital and handed out by an orderly. The toast was cold, the milk for the corn flakes warm; the stewed prunes in the dish looked as though someone had already tried to eat them, unsuccessfuly. The coffee was the dregs from the urn kept boiling for the hospital's night crew.

Overall, breakfast was no worse than lunch and dinner had been yesterday. One of Runner's earlier women had spent several days in the hospital. The patients received far better food than the prisoners.

He rejected everything, called the sergeant to order from the diner. The man ambled slowly over, stared at Runner for nearly thirty seconds. Then he spat, grimacing, and turned away without answering.

Runner felt the first surge of anger, forced himself to remain calm by breathing deep, breathing slowly. He turned to the sink, washed as best he could with the cheap soap supplied with the threadbare towel and washcloth, and tried to scrub the fur from his teeth with a finger. Yesterday's shirt was stiff beneath the arms when he pulled it on. Except for his shoes, everything he now wore would go into the trash the moment he reached home.

Twenty minutes later the sergeant returned to gather up the trays, heralding his coming by the crash of the locking bar. Runner jumped, the hackles on his neck rising, as he had jumped each time the bar dropped.

"Stand back from the door!"

He obeyed, smothering amusement as the sergeant

cracked the door just enough to reach in and grab the tray. As soon as the tray was through the crack he slammed the door shut, then straightened.

"Hey, Dads!" It was the youth who had been in the fight, his words distorted by his swollen mouth. "Why don't you an' me figger a way to crash out of this dump? You take the old man, you . . . dirty . . . rat!"

The boy in the next cell laughed and the two began a conversation, cursing the stupidity of the adult world that had put them here. The fighter was trying to regain his girl from a rival; the boy had been caught breaking into his teacher's house, intending to trash the place as revenge for flunking.

Runner ignored them, beginning the twenty minute series of exercises that started his every morning. There was no bar, but he concentrated on each movement in turn, straining each muscle until it popped, began to hurt. Sweat poured freely before he finished. He used the towel to soak up the excess, then stretched out on the cot again.

The bar crashed. Runner sat up as Monaghan appeared, accompanied by Cox.

"You took your time," he said.

"It's only 7:30," protested the agent. "Don't break my balls." He seemed much more tired, and several times broke off to yawn widely. "The DA doesn't like the idea of losing his prime and only suspect. It took a six AM phone call from a very important and very pissed off personage at Langley before he'd listen to reason."

"That was still an hour and a half ago."

"I had to wait in his living room while the man showered, shaved, dressed and read his goddamn paper as he ate breakfast. The bastard didn't even offer me coffee," he added bitterly.

Chief Forey was standing by the desk when they crossed the basement corridor; the sergeant brought out the envelope of Runner's valuables while he threaded his belt through its loops. He took time to compare the contents against the list he had signed, counting both bills and change.

"Professor, I want you to know this wasn't my idea." The chief shuffled from foot to foot like a guilty child. "The charges and all. I was only following orders."

Runner shrugged. "I understand."

"I know you do," said Forey, relieved. "We all have to follow orders."

"Not all of us," said Runner, turning away as Forey started to offer his hand.

The chief glared at the sergeant as he let his hand fall, while Cox appeared with Runner's outer wear. The patrolman had a city newspaper folded under his arm and offered it so Runner could read the headlines:

PROFESSOR CHARGED AS SLASHER
"He did it!" says dead woman's best friend.
Ex-war hero Colonel James Runner was arrested yesterday morning, charged with the brutal knife slaying of Sandra Blake only hours after allegedly committing the heinous crime. (More photos on page 3.)

"You should sue for libel, Jamie," said Monaghan.

"What's the point? The story is worded to say I've been charged with the murder, not that I did it. Who should I sue, Angie Gray?"

"At least make them publish a retraction."

"Which would appear on page six, seen by no one. It isn't worth the effort."

"Ah, I suppose you're right."

Monaghan cracked another yawn as Runner followed him into the basement corridor and then up to the first floor of the courthouse.

"We've set up a team in a motel four miles south of town, Jamie. They're bringing' in what we already have so you can get started right away."

"No."

The agent stopped short within the courthouse entrance. Beyond him the sky was blue, filled with drifting cloudbergs that towered into the stratosphere. There were no idle watchers waiting in the street to see Runner's return to freedom, no photographers or cameramen. The sun gave promise of providing warmth as the day spun on.

"I'm going home," explained Runner, before Monaghan could protest further. "I'm going to do just what the district attorney did. Bathe. Have breakfast."

"But—"

"I stink, Monaghan. I don't like smelling myself. I suggest you go someplace and do the same."

He sighed. "All right, Jamie, though Washington most definitely will not be happy. One hour, and I'll come by your place to get you."

"I'll drive myself when I'm ready." There was no emotion in his flat statement, but Runner's jaw was set.

Monaghan sighed again. "Jesus! You're as stubborn as an Irishman."

The agent's car was in a No Parking zone directly in front of the courthouse. He opened the door for Runner, ignored village traffic ordinances driving him to his apartment. He couldn't resist a last plea as Runner got out of the car.

"Two hours, Jamie. Be there no later, please."

The strain was telling on him; Runner knew how much it cost Monaghan to add the last word. He nodded, closing the car door, and turned to see the building superintendent staring at him.

"Mr. Sidney." He nodded again.

"Perfesser."

The man backtracked to quickly get out of his way. Runner ran up the stairs to his apartment, discarding the jacket as he brought out his keys. Inside, he left a trail of clothes to the bedroom, shucking everything before he went in to draw the bath. Steam billowed quickly and he slid into the still-filling tub, closing his eyes as heat suffused his muscles. For the next thirty minutes he thought of nothing at all.

An hour later, skin glowing, Runner came down to his Mercedes sports car and aimed it for a dairy on the edge of town that had its own coffee shop. There he was conscious of staring eyes as some of the customers glanced at their papers, comparing the reality with the printed image. He ignored them.

Hunger appeased, for the moment Runner felt renewed. But almost immediately a cloud passed in front of the sun, and with the shadow came the realization that Sandy was . . .

Dead.

*　　*　　*

The motel was three years old, a sprawling two-story affair with wings reaching toward the woods behind the highway. The team had taken over the first floor of one wing. Runner pulled into the space next to Monaghan's car and was met by the agent, who had been watching for him from the window.

"A special group has been set up to handle this investigation, Jamie. We report directly to the National Security Council. We have boys and girls from all the agencies involved in Intelligence: Central, Defense, the Criminal Division of Justice, the National Security Agency. Hell, there's even a honcho from Immigration and Naturalization, and State sent over somebody from the Bureau of Politico-Military Affairs. Don't ask me why," he added, in the lament of all lesser cogs in the wheels of bureaucracy.

Half-a-dozen men and women were in the first room Monaghan took him into, sorting through cartons marked with the names of one or another of the murder victims. Computer printouts were stacked in the center of the two beds and on the floor, and a coffee maker bubbled gently to itself on the dresser.

Runner stopped short when he saw that several of the cartons were marked with Sandy's name.

"You work fast," he said, bluntly.

"All stops are open," said Monaghan. "Washington wants answers, and fast."

A woman opened one of Sandy's cartons and began to dictate a list of the contents to a man taking shorthand. Heads looked up at Runner's entrance, then went back to what they were doing.

"Most of this stuff just got here ten minutes ago," said Monaghan. "A team's goin' through Blake's apartment in Washington. They'll be feedin' the computer in Langley, and by this afternoon the printouts will come out of the FBI tie line in Boston. They'll ship it up to us by chopper."

He ushered Runner out and into a room down the line. It was empty, although a cork board had been set up against the wall. Eight-by-ten glossies of the eight victims lined the top of the board, as they had been in life; newspaper clippings of the various deaths were pushpinned below.

"You'll work here, Jamie." Monaghan indicated a comfortable chair. Runner sucked in breath.

"Just what do you expect me to find?"

"I don't know. Somebody ordered four people killed to insure that four of our agents died. Jamie, you have somethin' . . . a talent, I guess. Or good luck. You spotted trouble, in the field, back in Battalion, before anybody else knew anything was wrong. That's why you were so good. That's why the high command practically crapped purple when you resigned."

He eyed the bed with longing, his eyes reddened and puffy; his face was haggard and drawn.

"We're bettin' you can find the connection between these people, Jamie. Lord knows we've struck out. Study these eight people, try to become them."

"And if I fail? If I prove not to be the supernatural genius you think I am?"

"Well, we'll have tried. We'll try something else. All along the line we're gonna give it our best shot."

Monaghan left, and a moment later another agent came in with a stack of eight manila file folders, dropping them on the motel room's combination desk-dresser. Runner stared at them for a moment, and then at the row of pictures; his gaze stopped at the last. On Sandy . . .

He sighed, and picked up the top folder from the stack.

*   *   *

That was Friday: the beginning of four days of intensive study into the lives of eight people who hadn't known each other, except for their twins. His eyes were bleary; a woman came and administered eye drops. After twenty hours he dropped across a bed for four hours of sleep that ended when Monaghan came in with a fresh pot of coffee.

During those four days Runner never left the room. Food came on trays from the motel coffee shop, barely better than jail fare. He hadn't thought to pack a bag. Monaghan went to his apartment, brought back clean underwear, shirts, socks to last a week. From time to time the Irishman came in to drop into a chair, sometimes without words. Sometimes Runner welcomed his voice.

"Who is coordinating this?" Runner asked. "Langley?"

"No. National Security, through Fort Meade."

"Just how big is this special group?"

"Counting clerks, at the moment about two hundred."

Runner went back to sifting through the vast accumulation of material. There were histories, medical records, school records, personnel files. There were evaluations and critiques and fitness reports. In one box was a Fifth Grade essay, "What America Means to Me." It was graded C+.

From time to time he lowered the material in hand to

study the photograph of the subject. All eight had been caught at moments of laughter: They were alive and filled with the joy of life.

Runner remembered Monaghan's description of sliding into his brother's empty mind. He emptied his own thoughts, tried to do the same: Nothing. He knew Sandy, could bring her to life; he closed his eyes and heard her voice, felt her presence, the brush of her hand across his cheek.

Tuesday: Day five. The coroner released Sandy's body for burial; Sam had arrived the day before, flown by air force courier to Logan airport in Boston. It was to be a double funeral; Runner left the motel early to return to his own apartment to dress.

Necks craned and eyes stared as he entered the church alone. Angie Gray sat in the first pew by herself; Sandy's friends occupied the second and third pews. There were more than a hundred people, including Cassell and Mabry and half a dozen of Monaghan's group.

Runner slipped into one of the last pews and shut off his mind when the service started. Commotion in front made him come back to reality. He slipped out quickly, walked hurriedly to his car. He had decided against going to the cemetery for the final empty ritual.

Back at the motel, still dressed in suit and overcoat, he clapped his hands atop his head and closed his eyes. He heard the door open; the person left again. Runner wasn't thinking; thinking would be too painful.

But at last he sighed and stood to remove overcoat and coat, then picked up a list of the articles found in Sam Blake's apartment. He scanned the familiar lines quickly . . . came back to one.

> *. . . items on coffee table: miscellaneous newspapers;* Time *magazine;* Reader's Digest; *horoscope; paperback,* Sun Signs, *Linda Goodman; book,* Love Signs, *Linda Goodman . . .*

Runner read the list again, rubbing his mouth. Then he reached for another of the inventory sheets. Somewhere in it . . .

> *Astrology magazine; horoscope chart . . .*

Sam Blake had believed in astrology, deeply. Sandy had laughed the first time she came to Runner's apartment and saw his large library that concentrated on the occult. She had said she didn't believe, but had consented to Runner's casting her horoscope.

"James, you can't really believe that the lives of people alive today are influenced by the chance position of the stars two thousand years ago!"

"I don't know," he had admitted. "Astrology was the first science, alchemy the second. I know astronomers decry the occult, but there are forces that influence the lives of men. Call them God, the Fates, whatever you wish."

Sandy's chart was still on his desk, unfinished. There seemed no point to finishing it now. He regretted allowing himself to be sidetracked.

Runner rifled through the inventory lists again. Either occult papers and charts or astrology magazines were listed under at least one of each pair of twins; in two cases both had horoscopes listed.

Twenty minutes later the people next door were busy digging into their cartons, telephoning Langley, where Sam Blake's belongings were still held. Three of them came up with horoscopes bound in report covers.

Monaghan stood behind Runner's shoulder as he spread the reports on a bed and rapidly scanned them. He knew as soon as he opened the second, but he waited to finish the third before leaning back to make his announcement.

"This is it."

"Yeah?" Monaghan scratched his ear, perplexed. "Why? I'll give you three horoscopes is a bit much, Jamie, but what's the connection?"

"All three were cast by the same astrologer."

"How can you tell?"

"Look them over."

Monaghan picked up the three reports, flipped them through. The charts at the beginning of each report were pre-printed, but added symbols and notations made each different. He shook his head.

"I don't see it. You say they're by the same person, but there's no identification on them. Not even the name of the person they were made for. Different typewriters, too, different paper. Even different covers."

Relieved to have the tedious search through the minutiae of eight people done with, Runner stretched widely, dragging out the moment by picking up a coffee container. It was cold; he made a face.

"An astrologer identifies himself everytime he draws a chart, Monaghan. Imprints his signature, just as you identify yourself when you sign your name on a check. He draws the symbols the same way each time, and uses the same phrasing in his report and his predictions." He picked up the three reports. "These are nicely done. The work of a professional. They seem different only because they were typed by services in different cities. There are labels inside the back covers."

Monaghan flipped them open in turn. "New York, Washington, D.C., Boston. This fella gets around the east coast." He closed the reports. "I'll get on the horn, Jamie, but do you have any idea who our man might be?"

He shook his head. "I don't know many practicing astrologers—a few, by reputation. None in person."

After Monaghan left, Runner stretched out on the bed and closed his eyes. It seemed only a moment until the agent returned, but a glance at his watch told him nearly two hours had passed.

"The New York outfit hung up on our man," said the agent, "but Baltimore cooperated. It's a one-woman shop and she only did the one job, for a Madame Olana."

Runner blinked. "Olana rings a bell. Nothing more. Did you get an address?"

"A hotel. Boston was better. The service there does a lot of work for Madame Olana Venedris, although we had to apply muscle before she'd crack her files. The address is on Holden, in Dorchester."

"Now what?" asked Runner, sitting up.

"This is still in your area, Jamie. So I guess you go to Boston."

SIX

Runner angled the Mercedes around a plodding twenty-year old Buick, ignoring the look of outrage from the plump gray-haired woman driver, and cut back in just in time to avoid a lumbering hay truck that filled the air with the stink of manure. The driver honked, his load swaying precariously as he swung the truck over onto the shoulder.

The curving, two-lane highway fell as it crossed the state line, passing from the Berkshire hills into the Pioneer Valley of Massachusetts. From there the sports car cut east on US 202 and Massachusetts 2. The tires hummed noisily on the pavement, but the sound was muted by the rush of wind past the half-cracked window as Runner held the speed at seventy.

The Mercedes was built for speed, restless and querulous under the plodding granny-limits mandated by the fifty-five miles-per-hour laws. Below sixty, the engine grumbled to itself beneath its exhaust breath, although it was too well-behaved an instrument to embarrass its driver in public. Still, at seventy, the little car was just beginning to feel good. It could hold these curves at one hundred ten, if only given a chance.

The day was deceptively warm, the sky a clear azure blue, the ambient air temperature rising to a comfortable seventy-eight. Runner had discarded his jacket at the start of the trip. Only the sere stalks of dead cornfields on both sides of the road and the last remnants of autumn's leaves clinging futilely to the dead-gray branches of weary trees marked the true season of the year.

Runner felt good, both physically and mentally. It was the first time in six days he had felt close to human. Leaving the scene of tragedy was like escaping from prison . . . not the prison of the decrepit jail in the basement of the old courthouse, but from a private prison of the soul.

His mood sunk again as he thought of Sandy. The memory was still sharp, but her image no longer overwhelmed everything else. Only half his mind had concentrated on the search through the records of the murdered intelligence agents and their twins. The other half saw her, standing there to one side of the motel room, silent and with puzzlement on her face.

His spirit lifted again as he forced Sandy from his thoughts. Runner was alone in the car. A repacked bag rested on the luggage shelf behind the seat and photocopies of the three horoscopes cast by Madame Olana were in the trunk, secure and concealed. Perhaps the horoscopes were only a coincidence, but closing his eyes, it was almost as though the first on the inventory lists had been written in letters of fire, shouting: Look at me! Look at me!

Maybe it wasn't a logical conclusion, but he had not

relied on logic in making the connection. Perhaps Monaghan was right, perhaps he did have a talent in such matters. A sixth sense. Runner had never given particular credence to the various manifestations of ESP—telepathy, clairvoyance, telekinesis. They smacked of witchery. Of charlatanism.

Was Madame Olana a charlatan? Possibly. He would know as soon as he saw her, saw how she operated.

ESP . . . psychic powers. He wished he had given more attention to the whole field of parapsychological phenomena. The evidence he had seen was empirical, neither proving nor disproving the truth of the experimenters' claims. But there did seem to be strong psychic bonds between close relatives, even lovers.

And devoted scientists, in the United States and around the world, were giving the field serious study. There were rumors of government-sponsored research, although usually denied. To the establishment mind, scientific or government, there was something embarrassing about the whole subject.

A long-forgotten news story popped out of the filing cabinet of Runner's memory. In 1959 the Navy investigated telepathy as a means of communication between submarines using the nuclear sub, Nautilus. The story was denied. A few years later, the Russians admitted to at least one experiment using a mother rabbit and her newborn litter. The infants were killed, one at a time, and each time the mother, thousands of miles away, registered severe trauma on an EEG.

Positive results. There should have been follow-up experiments, but none that were publicized.

The subject was interesting, now that he thought about it. Once this matter was done with, Runner decided to follow up the current experiments in para-psychology.

If his sixth sense was a manifestation of the latent powers of his mind, he wanted to know. He wanted to be able to control it.

The Mercedes sped east, through Acton and Leo-minster and the small towns along the way, slowing occasionally as traffic clogged near interchanges and larger population centers. Runner's concentration threaded the little car through traffic with the ease of long experience, yet his attention was elsewhere. Three times something told him to slow to fifty-five, although the road was clear; once he passed a radar trap around the next corner, and twice came up on state police cruisers at the side of the road. He had always been a fast driver, yet not once in his life had he received a ticket.

At the thought, Runner laughed. Perhaps there *was* something to ESP.

Monaghan had stayed behind, wrapping up opera-tions in the motel. Most of the clerks shipped in at overnight notice would be back in Fort Meade, Mary-land, by tomorrow, serving the National Security Agency. They had been co-opted to Monaghan's group, but for the moment there was nothing more for them to do.

The redhead agent would join Runner in Boston this evening, where both had rooms reserved at the Ritz-Carlton. Runner was to check in with Monaghan after his initial contact with Madame Olana.

They knew more about the astrologer now. Runner's file-memories came up with the name of a secretary at the American Association of Astrologers, and a twenty minute phone call gave him almost more information than he wanted.

According to her official biography, Olana Venedris was young, still in her twenties. She had first appeared on the national scene five years ago, contributing tidbits to *The Gnostica News*, an occultist tabloid out of Minneapolis that was no longer in business. Her items were witty and pleased the editor. Within three months she graduated to a regular column, gossip oriented, that specialized in warning of big troubles looming along love's highway for the rich, the famous. Soon hers was the most popular feature in the paper, the faithful believing every word she printed. There was talk that a national syndicate wanted to move the column into the daily newspapers.

It never happened. Suddenly, about a year before the paper folded, the column was dropped. That was three years ago. At the same time Olana began to call herself Madame Olana, and she started giving personal consultations to a select list of distinguished and important people. Her initial entry into the world of the rich and the famous came through her show-business contacts: a fading matinee idol, a downer-addicted rock star and an alcoholic best-selling author.

In less than a year, however, Olana abandoned the entertainment industry, severing relations with the people who gave her a start. Her new clients were personages from the fields of national and international high finance and from the upper ranks of government.

Now it was said her only movie star was a man who commanded five million dollar fees, and then produced and distributed the films through his own companies. It was widely known that he considered himself ready to enter the political arena. The secretary breathlessly gave it to Runner as the best of words that Olana read every script submitted to the movie star, advising him on which roles to accept.

"Her clients trust her implicity, Dr. Runner."

Now, after a meteoric rise in prestige, the secretary passed on the rumor that some of the highest-placed men in Washington were afraid to make a major move without first consulting the stars through Madame Olana.

"Only men?" asked Runner.

"Why, now I think of it, yes." The secretary clucked her tongue. "Now isn't that strange? I can't think of a single woman who consults her. Of course," she added, cattily, "she *is* beautiful. I suppose it's the gypsy blood. I did tell you Madame Olana is gypsy, didn't I? A true Romany, I've heard. You know, the ones who ignore international borders and niceties like paying taxes and registering births. You know the type. Stunning while they're young, but fat and frumpy by forty."

He grinned as he thanked her, drawing a scowl from Monaghan, and jotted down Madame Olana's unlisted Boston phone number. He called immediately; the woman who answered spoke in a throaty cultured voice that should have formed ice crystals in the long distance equipment.

"Unless referred by a present client, Madame Olana is unable to consult with new applicants."

Runner identified himself before she could hang up. There was an instant thaw, throaty contralto rising up the scale to an almost girlish trill.

"Dr. Runner! Oh, dear! I'm sure Madame Olana

will be delighted to see *you*, at any time. Are you in Boston now, doctor?''

''I'm coming in this afternoon.''

''Eight o'clock? No, I'm sorry; Madame Olana has a dinner engagement. And, dear me, she is tied up all this afternoon . . . could you make it at eleven?''

''Eleven would be fine, Miss—''

''Twilty. Agatha Twilty. I'm Madame Olana's secre—Oh damn!'' The sudden explosion was most definitely not cultured and ladylike. ''Excuse me, doctor,'' she added, lamely.

''Is something wrong, Miss Twilty?''

''Darn it, I want to meet you, but I have an engagement I just can't break. I've followed your career for the longest time. I read your paper on 'Comparisons of Lunar Influences on the Part of Fortune,' and was so disappointed you weren't able to give it in person at last year's annual meeting of the AAA.''

''Well, perhaps I'll be in Boston long enough to pay Madame Olana a second visit.''

Runner murmured a few more niceties, assured Miss Twilty he had the address, and laughed as he hung up. He shared the joke with Monaghan, but the agent only stared at him, then sighed and shook his head.

''Jamie, you're a nerd.''

''I beg your pardon?''

''Mind you, nobody ever suspected you of bein' less than a man, but Jesus! The women who wanted to fall into the sheets for you . . . Christ, I knew a hundred guys who cried in their beer at what you passed up. You walked right by them all without tossin' a look.''

''Women wanted me?'' he said, dumbly.

''You can't be that much of a jerk!''

"Sorry." He shrugged. "I suppose I was. Then."

"Yeah, you've changed. In Nam we never could understand why you went for those Saigon hookers, when you could have played the embassy circuit. Christ, the finest birds in the world were ready an' eager, but you ignored them all."

As Monaghan walked away with another sigh, Runner was left with a new image of himself. A ladykiller? He laughed again, the first time his mood had broken since learning of Sandy's death.

The good mood was still with him as he passed MIT and then took the Harvard Bridge across the Charles River, switching from Massachusetts Avenue to Boylston Street. A few minutes later, after fighting city traffic, Runner pulled the Mercedes into the garage of the Ritz-Carlton, surrendering his bag to an obsequious bellboy with silver hair and impeccable manners.

The Ritz-Carlton lobby was hushed, despite the presence of Halston-dressed young matrons and a gaggle of top-heavy girls who could have been on their way to the pool area of the Beverly Hills Hotel, rather than toward whatever destination their tanned lithe limbs were directed. Girls and matrons eyed Runner with unabashed interest as he crossed the lobby to the desk. He grinned at the young clerk who appeared to take his registration and caught a blank and cold stare in return.

The spell was broken; he was back in the Ritz-Carlton, in well-mannered old Boston. The clerk studied Runner's handwriting five seconds longer than necessary, lip curving upward as he turned to the reservation file; and then his supercilious manner turned to limpid warmth as he turned back again.

"Yes, Dr. Runner. We have the reservation. Welcome back to the Ritz-Carlton."

The room was a suite on the sixth floor, complete with fireplace, overlooking the Public Gardens. The bellboy offered to light a fire, even thought it was afternoon and balmy. Runner declined.

After unpacking, he went down to the dining room for a late lunch. He was alone in the hushed reaches of the room, the elderly waiter hovering discreetly near. He finished his sandwich and coffee quickly, and went out into the afternoon. Boston was beautiful. It had always been one of his favorite cities.

He crossed Arlington and passed through the Gardens to Boston Common, pausing from time to time to breathe in the air, to watch the young people. The swan boats were put up for the season: a bleak sight momentarily depressing. Runner had come here a hundred times since his childhood and on each visit thought that a ride on the ungainly yet graceful boats would be a cap to the day's pleasure.

Something had always interfered, however; and now that he had the time, the calendar was against him.

On the way back he passed an occultist book shop which dug up most of the back issues of *The Gnostica News* that contained Olana Venedris' column. The temperature fell as he returned to the hotel, just beating dusk.

In his suite, he settled down to read all of the astrologer's columns, rereading items that might be pertinent and fixing them in his memory. Then he scanned the rest of the papers, rapidly reading half-a-dozen articles on telepathy and the psychic bond.

It was eight by the time he finished. He dressed in a conservative dark suit and took a cab to the Cafe Budapest. The temperature was down to the low forties and still falling. The sky was beginning to cloud; snow was in the air.

The restaurant was thronged, but Runner had called earlier, was an old and valued patron. Tourists and unknowns stared with jealousy as he was ushered past the velvet rope and taken to one of the finest tables. The manager sat with him through the first course, beaming when Runner nodded approval at the wine.

After dinner Runner decided to walk back to the Ritz-Carlton to freshen up before his meeting with Madame Olana.

The taxi dropped him at the corner of Holden five minutes before eleven. Holden proved to be a narrow two block street just off Columbus and on the flats below the Dorchester Heights. Five-and-six story apartment buildings, good solid middle-class structures, twenty or thirty years old, lined both sides of the street.

Runner found the address: It was the only house on the block, a town house much older than its neighbors. From the architecture, it might have dated to the Federal period, the early nineteenth century.

The house had four storeys and was cut from solid blocks of stone. In the night, it seemed gray, with darker gray trimming. Then carriage lamps at either side of the entrance showed the trim to be a deep wedgewood blue.

A black-apinted wrought iron fence circled the property, protecting the skirts of the house from contamina-

tion by its twentieth century neighbors. The narrow
stretch between fence and house was brick paved.
Three low stone steps worn in the center led up to the
white-painted door; the gate in the fence seemed tacky
under his fingers when he opened it, despite the temperature that was now into the thirties.

Runner searched for the bell, found an antique pull
that was only half as old as the house. A deep bong
sounded somewhere in the depths of the house and a
moment later the door opened, but the opening was
blocked by the massive shoulders of the black giant
who stood there.

"Dr. Runner? Please come in. Madame Olana is
expecting you."

The black was three inches taller than Runner, but
built like a professional football player: a linebacker.
He outweighed Runner by at least eighty pounds.

The two men studied each other, sizing the other up
as a possible opponent. The black's nose was considerably flatter than it had been at birth and his upper lip
was lined with a network of faint scars. He introduced
himself as Ramsey.

Wearing an undertaker's black suit, white shirt,
black tie, he moved against the foyer wall, crowding a
steam radiator. Runner had to turn sideways to sidle
past him, through an arch and into the main hallway.

Ramsey took Runner's overcoat and opened a set of
sliding doors while Runner scanned the hallway. It was
narrow, carpeted with a worn Persian rug runner in
shades of blue that matched the walls, and undoubtedly
matched the exterior color scheme of the house as well.
A dark wood staircase led into the upper reaches.

"Please wait in the library, doctor. Madame Olana will join you there."

Runner moved past Ramsey, into a tall room furnished in Regency style. Floor to ceiling bookcases lined three of the walls; an antique sofa, enameled in blue and upholstered in blue and orange silk, was against the opposite wall. A white and gold coffee table sat before it. Another antique table served as Madame Olana's desk; fragile chairs were placed behind it and to either side.

The room was in the best of taste; Runner was sure the antiques were genuine. Papers were scattered across the desk, mostly charts in progress, were the only sign of disorder. A crystal ball served as a paperweight, but another, larger one on the coffee table seemed meant for use.

Above the sofa were paintings, symbolic pictures of the ancient astrological planets. A framed collage of occultist manuals and a poster of old treatises formed a cabinet door three shelves high in the center of one set of bookshelves.

Runner stepped to the nearest shelf, scanned the titles with one eye. Most of them were in his own library, although there were first editions he did not have and fine bindings that added considerably to their value. The impression of the house and the library was one of quiet wealth, unostentatiously used.

Sucking in short, flat breaths of air, Runner tuned his attention to the rest of the house. He moved along the side wall far enough to see through the sliding doors. No one was there. Still, the crawling feelings moved up his spine, the hackles on his neck refused to flatten.

Every nerve, every sense he possessed, whether normal or paranormal, screamed loudly.

Trouble.

Get out, now!

He moved to the center of the room, waiting. The solid stone walls of the house muffled any sounds, except for a creak that might have been two hundred-year old floor joists shifting beneath someone's weight.

Runner was alert, adrenalin pumping into his bloodstream. The first warning signals came when he entered the street, so intense he had spun once, expecting to find someone tailing him. The street was empty and the feeling faded, although never leaving completely as he approached the house, was ushered into the library.

Time stopped, as it had when he had lunged at Monaghan. Runner could feel his heart swelling in his chest, readying for a systolic beat. He was aware of a trembling muscle in his thigh, of cords stretched taut in anticipation of sudden orders to move. His hearing picked up a faint hum, puzzled over it for ten seconds, then his mind decided it was a refrigerator coming to life somewhere.

The black was there, filling the opening between the sliding doors; the top of his head brushed the lintel. There had been no warning of his coming, no sound to give him away. He stared at Runner, lids lowered to hood his pupils and conceal his thoughts. A bulge beneath his jacket was a gun, and Runner knew he carried a sap in his back pocket. He could visualize the coins weighing the black's pocket.

"Is something wrong, doctor?"

Runner forced himself to relax, let the air out of his lungs. "No. You . . . startled me."

He assimilated the information, nodded once and stepped aside. "Madame Olana, doctor."

SEVEN

A black-haired woman materialized in the space
Ramsey had vacated: Olana Venedris was dressed con-
servatively, perhaps to appear older than her age, in a
silk sheath of deep lavender. Her hair was drawn back
and styled severely, framing an oval face. Only the
barest hint of makeup highlighted a complexion so pale
as to seem bloodless. Eyes as deep in color as Runner's
sparkled back highlights of the artificial illumination.
The full voluptuous mouth was painted blood red, the
only color in her face.

She came into the library, offering her hand and
smiling. "Doctor Runner? This is an honor."

As she approached, Runner stared, almost trans-
fixed. A single strand of pearls circled her throat. She
wore an antique cameo on her breast, the head of a girl.
It was white against a lavender two shades paler than
the dress. An amethyst circled by diamonds glittered on
her right hand, the only other jewelry in her costume.

Runner blinked, suddenly, and awkwardly accepted
her hand. He felt like a small child, awed before visit-

ing royalty. The heat of his embarrassment reddened his ears.

"Uh . . ." He swallowed. "Madame."

She wore a perfume that hinted at sexual mysteries as ancient as the secrets of the stars; the musk put the lie to her outward appearance. He studied her carefully, seeing not the young woman who in a few short years had risen to become confidant to some of the most powerful men in the country, but the gypsy beneath the surface. The gyspsy was there, looking out of her eyes, laughing with her voice, vibrantly alive behind the mask and the costume.

Olana Venedris was woman raw: wild and untamed. The urbane setting, the designer-original clothing, were wrong. She should have been wearing brilliant colors, swirling skirts, the costume of the uncivilized ancient race of Romany. She belonged in a gypsy camp, dancing barefoot to the music of savage violins as she clapped out the beat of a primitive and lust-driven rythm. The long tresses should be free to flow with her wild dancing, to form a dark cloud framing the blood-red lips and the feral white teeth. Those primitive emotions should be firing young men, those dark eyes reflecting campfires as they threw off fire of their own.

The astrologer smiled, recognizing Runner's discomfiture, and reclaimed her fingers. Runner moved back a half pace.

"Thank you for seeing me on such short notice."

Why was his heart beating so wildly? Runner's blood roared in his ears, heated in animal-response to the lust the astrologer deliberately excited. The smartly-styled dress had been tailored to conceal the full curves of her body, the voluptuousness that was sex incarnate; but he saw through the fabric, saw her naked as she intended, arms thrown wide in lustful greeting, pelvis thrust forward, demanding to be impaled on a male standard.

His palms were wet with perspiration; he could see dark stains beneath her arms. She was aroused as he. He suppressed an insane urge to drop to one knee before this imperious woman. He breathed in her musk, barely masked by hundred dollar an ounce perfume, and managed to swallow an inane comment.

Forgotten completely were the warnings of danger that had come as he approached this house.

She smiled again. "Thank you for coming . . . James? Please, let's put aside formalities. I am Olana and you are James . . . or do you prefer something else?"

"James, please." Runner managed a self-conscious laugh.

She moved past him, to the sofa, and sat, carefully arranging her skirt. Then she looked up at him, touched the sofa by her side.

"Please, James, sit here."

Runner obeyed her gesture, blood singing again and fighting an almost uncontrollable urge to grin. He felt like a teenager making his first illicit approach to love, although he moved away from her as he sat, trying to keep as wide a distance as he could.

"Well." She leaned back. "I hate to sound as though I think you belong with the ancients and the graybeards, James Runner, but I have followed your career ever since I was a little girl."

He laughed with her, and lied: "I can't say the same,

but I have followed you and your rather remarkable career ever since your column began in *The Gnostica News*."

"You flatter me." She gave a conspiratorial wink. "If you did read 'Star Tales,' I hope you didn't believe any of the nonsense I printed. Most of it was only puffery for the paper."

"But entertaining. Which was its purpose. You gave the readers what they wanted, what they paid for."

"Yes . . . but entertaining the great public is not why I was placed on this earth. And from your own work, I know you don't dismiss the stars so readily. What does bring you to Boston, James?"

"To the city, business. That is taking care of itself, as it turns out. I also knew I was going to have some free time, and when I heard you were here, decided I could think of no better way to spend an evening than in the company of a respected fellow student of the stars."

His words pleased her; she beamed.

"Would you like me to cast your horoscope?"

"If you have the time. I'd be delighted."

"For you, I will make the time."

There was a faint hint of accent in her voice, evident for the first time as she let her arm drop across the back of the sofa. Runner was aware of her fingers, only an inch away from touching him. He could feel her body heat rising, even through his jacket.

"What is your natal date, James—no. Don't tell me. Let me guess."

Olana studied him more closely, pursing her lips. Runner felt his blood heating again.

"At first appearance, surface impressions, one would think you a Pisces . . . or a Virgo. You seem to be studious, perhaps cold-hearted. You are the type to keep your emotions in control, under restraint. That is not just a quick judgment," she added. "You have that reputation."

"I know." He shook his head, remembering Sandy's words. "Lately I've been hearing a great deal of what others think of me. What else do they say?"

"That you are brilliant, even a genius. And very brave, James. Your war record reads like something out of a storybook. This is not an age of heroes."

"I never felt heroic."

"I suppose heroes never do, at least not while they're doing whatever it is that makes them heroes."

She withdrew her hand; Runner knew relief, and then knew shame at the feeling.

"Surface appearances are often deceptive," Olana continued. "I think that is true in your case, James. I've met a few people who claim to know you." She mentioned several astrologers with whom Runner had corresponded at various times. "They thought alike that you were born under one of the cold signs, but now that I see you, I know they were wrong."

"What is my sign?" he said, smiling.

"You were born under fire." She flicked a long fingernail across her bottom teeth. "Yes, but with a cold influence beneath it. Sagittarius, but with Pisces rising."

"Right you are."

"Yes. Cold on the surface, but underneath you're a seething cauldron. Ready to explode. Highy energetic and single-minded, but too much in restraint. You try to keep your emotions under lock and key."

"I suppose you're right." The smile didn't come as

easily. "I do think of myself as being in ctonrol."

She closed her eyes. "The date is . . . in December. Early in the month, very early. The first? No, but not the second, either."

Her eyes opened. "That doesn't make sense."

This time he did laugh. "I was born on the stroke of midnight."

"Ah, that explains it." She returned the smile.

"I'm told my head popped into the world seconds before the hour," Runner added. "But the rest of me came out after the toll. I didn't draw breath or let out my first squawl until the second. For years my parents argued over which should be the date. Mother wanted the first, but Father registered the bith certificate for the second."

"He was right," she said, firmly. "Before midnight you were still part of your mother's body, still wrapped in her essense. You had no life of your own. It was not until you drew breath that your life began." She relaxed. "I know your natal year. I'll start on your chart tomorrow."

"Please, don't make it a special project—don't take time from your regular clients."

Her fingers walked along the sofa again as she smiled. Runner colored, flinching as one digit reached daintily to touch him. The finger stroked his arm.

"This . . . will be a very special project."

Ramsey filled the library door, although she had given no signal heard by Runner. Perhaps the black had been waiting, just out of sight but within earshot.

The thought annoyed him. Angered him.

Runner yanked his hand back to his lap, aware he had been about to return her caress.

"Madame?"

"Brandy, please, Ramsey."

The black giant nodded and disappeared. He returned in less than a minute with a tray bearing two brandy snifters and a pair of snifter-warmers with candles, and a bottle of Remy-Martin.

"You do take brandy, James?"

"Thank you, yes."

Ramsey arranged glasses and warmers on the coffee table, filled the snifters and lit the candles. Then he retired with the tray, this time closing the sliding doors.

"A toast," said Olana, taking one of the glasses and offering it to Runner. "To us, James."

"To us as what?"

She shrugged. "As good friends, if nothing more."

He drank with her, sipping at the fiery liquid. The room was much too warm, the animal presence of her body much too disturbing. Runner tried to remember why he had come to this house.

"Do you study the Tarot, James?" asked Olana, placing her glass on the table. "Do you believe in the cards?"

"A reading is only as good as the reader," he said.

"And a good reader should be a true psychic."

"Otherwise it becomes only a parlor game."

"Ture enough." She studied him. "Do you consider yourself a psychic?"

"I don't know," he said, truthfully.

"Have you had . . . experiences?"

"The only answer to that is the same: I just don't know. Maybe. Once or twice. Maybe not."

"I think I'm psychic, James."

Olana rose with those words and crossed to the

bookshelves, opening the cabinet. She came back with an outsized deck of Tarot cards. The deck was very old, on heavy vellum rather than card stock. The pictures and devices were printed from wood blocks, then hand-colored.

"I'd like to read for you."

"The *Grand Tarot Belline?*"

"You do know your Tarot."

Runner held out his hand and Olana gave him the deck to examine. He handled it carefully, admiringly, as he looked through the suites.

"A beautiful copy. Early nineteenth century?"

"Supposedly," said Olana. "The auction gallery in London dates it to 1820. The provenance has it a copy made by a student of Mademoiselle Lenormande. It better be that old," she added. "I paid enough."

Runner smiled at the mention of the famous French psychic. Once fortune-teller to the Empress Josephine, Mademoiselle Lenormande was thrown repeatedly into the Bastille for being right in her predictions. Even Napoleon had consulted her . . . and jailed her.

"All early copies are supposed to be by students of Lenormande," he said. "It adds to their value."

"I think it is authentic," said Olana, "but authentic or not, it is beautiful. For you, James, I feel the Tree of Life pattern is best."

Runner nodded agreement. The Tree of Life pattern called for twenty-one cards: a row of three as base, three more built up vertically as trunk and five triads arranged around the trunk—on the bottom, Hopes balanced by Fears; above them, Realization balanced by Detriments; and over all, the crowning triad, Achievement.

Olana shuffled, offered the deck to Runner to be cut and rapidly began to lay out the pattern. The base, the Root of the Issue, produced the two of Cups, the High Priestess and the seven of Rods.

"Um. Affection, secrets, difficulties."

Before Runner could comment, Olana added the trunk, the Development, to the pattern: the four of Cups, the nine of Rods and the Last Judgment.

"Obligations, James," she said, studying the first six cards. "New opportunities, yet indecision. Someone new coming into your life." She looked up and smiled. "I hope that means me."

The lower left triad, Hopes, came next: the Heirophant, the six of Cups, the two of Swords. She quickly balanced it on the other side of the trunk with Fears: the Hanged Man, the nine of Swords and the Devil.

Olana paused again, shook her head. "Do you make anything of the pattern, James?"

Runner shrugged, uncomfortable with what he saw. "The picture isn't coming clear."

"No, it isn't," agreed the astrologer. "The pattern so far seems to suggest an unsettled situation. Trouble, aligned with fulfillment and balanced conflicts; yet on the other side we find guilt, expiation, something negative." She lowered the deck. "It's not the happiest portent, is it? Perhaps I should stop . . ."

Runner was hooked. He shook his head. "Continue, Olana."

The upper left triad, Realization, produced the six of Rods, the Empress and the World. On the other side, Detriments brought the ten of Rods, the four of Swords and the Sun.

Olana sucked in her breath, but before Runner could say anything, she moved on to lay out the crown, Achievement: the three of Rods, the six of Coins, the Hermit.

She raised her eyes, looked at him; she seemed stricken by the cards. "James . . ."

"Trouble," he said, bluntly."

"Yet there's an element of uncertainty," she said, puzzled. "I find the pattern . . . unclear. Where is the Lovers? It should be here, to balance the rest."

Suddenly she scooped up the cards, nervously putting the deck to one side, and sat back. "Well. Sometimes a reading produces a meaningful pattern. Other times it *is* only a parlor game."

Runner stared over his glass, breathing in the vapor of the brandy that was heated now by his body heat. He studied the astrologer across the rim, until Olana nervously looked away, reached to refill her glass.

The pattern of the Tarot was enigmatic, but it disturbed him deeply. He was sure that there was warning in the random lay of the cards, and he recalled his first reaction to this house.

Eight people had died: he must never forget that.

Four of them had been brutally murdered, and thus served as the instruments of death for the others. This woman had known at least three of the victims. If that was not more than sheer coincidence, there should be something here to tell him if he was on the right track.

He opened his mind, trying to banish all irrelevant thought as he stared at Olana Venedris. He was an open receptacle, a receiving station for her emotional broadcast, her moods, her feelings, her thoughts. She raised her head reluctantly, turned to meet his gaze.

Olana . . . glowed.

Runner could feel her psychic presence as a great burning fire; too great to be contained within her physical body. She overwhelmed everything: the physical contents of this room, the elements of this house. Her mind was a flame atop the column of fire, energy barely contained.

The glow of her being heated him dangerously; the fire baked into his flesh, into his bones. Runner could feel his blood singing as it began to boil, knew lust stirred uncontrollably in his loins.

He wanted her. He needed her.

His hand reached for Olana, trembling; she waited to accept him, commanding him with her will.

Runner fought sexual rut, the urge to paw the floor with cloven feet, to throw back his head and howl at the moon. Something primitive was loose—something he could neither contain nor control. The woman was too strong. Her emotions overpowered him, overwhelmed his senses.

He knew he was melting in the glow of Olana Venedris' psychic heat. Strength drained from his body, ran down his spine, dissipating into weakness. He fought her power with every erg of strength he could summon . . .

The lock holding their eyes broke. Runner looked away; his hand rested in his lap, trembling.

"More brandy, James?"

The woman acted as though nothing had happened, as if there had been no test of wills. She poured the brandy into Runner's glass, held it over the flame a moment for warmth. The glass was hot to his touch when he accepted it from her fingers.

The potent liquor lulled his senses. Runner was overheated. He drained the glass, lowered it to loosen his tie, then shrugged out of his jacket. Olana moved closer, opened the buttons of his shirt. An electric shock broke from her fingertips as she slipped them into the shirt, caressed his chest.

They kissed as he fumbled with her zipper, releasing the snaps of her brassiere. Her breasts fell from restraint, heavy against him as she rose onto his lap and pushed him back against the sofa. He had the momentary illusion of drowning, that her body had turned to a liquid that soaked into him, his very being, his soul. He slipped onto an ocean of limpid warmth, the stuff of Olana filling his lungs until he could no longer breathe. His body hurt with his need for her.

"I . . . admire you, James."

She breathed the words, nibbling at the lobe of his ear; her voice was a throaty growl that momentarily distracted him. It was familiar: Agatha Twilty, on the telephone.

"I admire few men, James," she said, hands moving freely over his back. "Most are weaklings, pretending to be strong. But there is no weakness in you. I can sense the rot in them, but your spirit is as strong as my own. We belong together."

Runner was intoxicated; it was more than the brandy. His eyes broke away from her and he tried to push her away.

"Olana! We're not children!"

She laughed. "That we are not. No child could appreciate what we have in each other. Come, James. To bed."

Her skirt was hiked up against him; she wore no other

underclothing but the bra. Runner's hands pushed against her thighs, caressed her buttocks, which were already heavy with the weight that would eventually bury her beauty. But at this moment the flesh filling his clutching fingers was sensual as she ground against him, destroying her dress.

Suddenly Olana sat up. She straightened her dress, freeing Runner to wipe his mouth with the back of his hand. His heart pounded heavily.

"You do find me . . . desirable?"

"Of course! You're a beautiful woman, Olana."

"Then what harm is there in enjoying each other?"

"None. None at all."

"Then you will stay the night," she said, firmly.

He surrendered completely. "If you wish."

"I wish." Olana stood. One stocking was twisted around her leg, and the dress would need extensive repairs before appearing again in public. Her breasts rose and fell heavily as she caught his hands, pulled Runner to his feet.

"Come to bed, James."

Olana released him and grabbed the brandy glasses, Runner the bottle. He followed her, nearly stubbing his toes against the track of the library door. What happened to his shoes? He looked back, saw them under the coffee table.

There was no memory of kicking them off.

And there was no sign of Ramsey as he follwed Olana up the stairs, to an immense bedroom on the third floor. The room was in shadows; he had no time to take it in before she put aside the glasses and came into his arms.

"Undress me. Quickly!"

Runner fumbled with her clothing and then with his own as Olana drew back a quilted coverlet. The bed was circular, immense—ten feet or more in diameter. She turned to him again while Runner stepped from his shorts. The heat of her body enveloped him as she tugged him toward the bed, grabbing a velvet pull rope as they fell. Draperies closed tightly about the bed, although indirect lighting gave just enough illumination to let them see each other.

Wrapped in the cylindrical closed world of the gypsy woman's lush bed, they made love, rising to climax together; and then they made love again. She made mewling sounds of pleasure as Runner fell across her body, depleted. For a time she held him close, accepting his weight as she uttered small endearments.

Olana shifted, rolled his weight from her body. They slept for awhile, the woman resting one hand on his hip. Then her body stirred, and she moved her hand down a few inches, bringing him back to life.

Runner reacted, reaching for her in his sleep. They moved together again and then he fell on his side, hand stroking Olana's hard nipple, cupping her breast. He looked up, blinking, and saw their shining bodies reflected overhead in a recessed mirror. Olana's hair tumbled in a wild circle that haloed her head, freed from restraint.

She turned to him again, sighing . . . moaning.

The night died, although there was no marking of time in the great circular bed. Runner's eyes opened, his time sense telling him something was wrong. He lay on his back, dried sweat coating his body, his feet tangled in the bedding.

Where was he?

Runner started to sit up, knowing momentary panic. Then he remembered. A smile touched his lips as he reached for the woman . . .

"Olana?"

He was alone in the bed. Alone in the room.

EIGHT

Runner froze.

Olana was gone.

Every sensory receptor he possessed shouted danger!

He knew the woman had left the room. The bed still carried the shape of her body, and a furrow across the sheet showed where she had crawled to the edge.

Completely awake and alert, Runner listened, but there was nothing to hear. The bed enclosure was effectively soundproofed by the circle of draperies.

The astrologer had been careful not to wake him, sure he was deep in the throes of sexual exhaustion. His seduction had been carefully planned and as carefully achieved. The repeated acts of sexual exercise had drained him of energy; she must have thought he would sleep through hell's eruption.

But the subconscious mind never sleeps, and Runner's subconscious was always on guard. Perhaps it was a sixth sense, a gift of God. Whichever, it had saved his life before.

He knew it had saved his life now.

Runner rolled onto his knees, rose to balance himself on the tips of his fingers while he opened his senses and listened with his mind. He probed beyond the room, into the house.

There were people below; none above. No one on this same level.

He touched the glowing aura that was Olana Venedris, recognizing it instantly. After last night, he would never forget that touch.

There were others, but he couldn't sense them in the same way he recognized Olana. Still, within minutes he was sure that five people were in the house. Another was a woman: perhaps Agatha Twilty, returned from her last evening's engagment. Logic said Ramsey would be one of the five. That left two strangers, unknown quantities.

Runner was in trouble; his mind sought a way out.

There was always a way out, though persons not blessed with the ability might be blind to it. In Nam, the path out of ambush was marked like a glowing red line when he closed his eyes.

It was the misfortune of the patrol that none of them shared Runner's ability. Even as he escaped, he knew guilt; and now he remembered the enigmatic Tarot pattern dealt by Olana. The card of expiation . . . could it be that this current problem would in some way lift his guilt over what had happened to the patrol?

For seven years Runner had lived with a feeling of culpability; he expected to carry the burden the rest of his life, even though the ambush had not been his fault. The gods of fortune frowned on those young Americans. Runner had only done his duty. But knowing he was blameless did nothing to ease the weight of their deaths.

A gap showed between two panels of the draperies: the place where Olana had left the bed.

Runner scuttled that way, thrust his head between the panels and peered into total darkness. Blinking, he swung his legs out of the bed and stood, then pulled the panels tight while he closed his eyes long enough to adjust to the new light level.

When he opened his eyes again, a faint glow to his right outlined a pale rectangle: French doors. They opened onto a shallow balcony overlooking Holden Street. Another dim glow across the room proved to be a three-panel dressing mirror.

Oriented, Runner opened the bed panels. The supports whirred softly in their overhead track. The new source of light was enough for him to pick out details, maneuver around the bulky furniture that stood as obstacles. There were chairs and at least one floor lamp, but he decided against risking the light.

He found his clothes heaped in the center of the floor where he had dropped them last night. One of Olana's stockings was tangled in his trousers; her other things had been removed.

Runner dressed quickly, pulling on his socks as he cast about for his shoes. Then he remembered they were still in the library, along with his suit jacket and his tie. Unless someone had carried them away.

Irritated, he searched the bedroom. No conscious thought guided his movements now; he acted from instinct, aware of the danger only two floors below.

How much time did he have?

Olana thought him asleep; there was time enough to prepare a surprise or two.

A void in his stomach told Runner he was hungry, but he pushed the thought aside. Adrenalin continued to pump into his blood stream. He knew he was burning calories at double or triple the normal rate, eating up the energy reserve stored in his body fats. It was fuel; if necessary, his body would burn the muscle tissue itself. He trusted his body to meet any demand he placed upon it. His body had never failed him; he could not comprehend such failure now.

He opened the door, cautiously. The third floor hall was in darkness, but light leaked up from the stairwell below. Runner listened, trying to sense out the people he had touched with his mind, but there was nothing.

A stair tread creaked.

Someone was coming up the stairs, silently. Moving slowly, as though afraid of giving warning.

Trouble.

Runner reacted almost instantly, pulling back into the bedroom. He eased the door shut, then spun, scanning the corners of the room. A floor-to-ceiling sliding door stood open in the far wall, spilling women's clothing.

He crossed the room quickly, pulled an armload of Olana's filmy finery from the hangers. The clothes resisted. He was forced to stop and lift the cluster of hangers from the wooden rod to which they were locked.

Whatever happened to the cheap wire hangers supplied by laundries? The kind that bent uselessly out of shape if you hung a T-shirt on them.

Runner's heart was beating at twice normal pace as he carried the armload of female clothes to the bed. There he yanked the sheet down and dumped them out, shaping them into a form roughly that of a man. He replaced the sheet. The sculpture bulged with unconvincing lumps.

He patted his creation smooth, until the dummy could pass for a sleeper in the dim illumination of the bed. The drapes closed when he tugged on the velvet cord. He moved away, flattening himself against the wall. When it opened, the massive panel would be between him and the skulker.

Runner knew the person on the stairs meant him no good.

He scanned the room again; his shirt was a pale blotch against the darker background of the wall and the floor. He considered moving, but too late. The antique door handle turned, uttering the very faintest of creaks as it was operated from the other side.

The door opened silently on well-oiled hinges. It swung in just far enough to let the intruder slip through the opening and into the bedroom.

Runner stopped breathing.

The man was small, dressed in dark clothing. A paler blotch floating in midair must have been his face.

Not big enough to be Ramsey.

Thirty seconds passed while the intruder adjusted his vision to the room. He hung in the door that time; then swung it shut, eased the panel into the frame. He didn't notice the slight rush of air as a partial vacuum was created on this side of the door. A current touched Runner's cheek, cool against his skin.

Another half minute passed while the intruder glued

himself to the wall, no more than six feet away from Runner. He watched only the bed, listening for signs of life from the occupant. If he had looked to his left, he could not have missed the bulk of the man he was after. Runner's hands were flat against the wall, ready to launch him into action if he was spotted.

The seconds dragged. His lungs ached with the strain of holding his breath. He permitted himself to blink no more than once every five seconds, afraid he'd miss the first move of the other.

The shadows of the bedroom were familiar now. The bed was a darker shape in the center of the room. Beyond it, Runner could easily make out the tall rectangle of the French windows. It seemed stronger than before, as though the world outside were lightening toward dawn.

The intruder moved. Runner was looking the wrong way. The man's hand came up from his side as he approached the bed, jutting forefinger unnaturally long. No one alive had one finger nearly twelve inches long.

The intruder's soles scuffed against the carpet. Runner took advantage of the slight sound to let the air trickle from his nostrils, breathe in again. The ache of oxygen-poor blood left his face and his joints as he moved after the other, thankful that he was in stockinged feet.

He was only two paces behind the intruder when the man caught a panel of the drapery and lifted it. For the next five seconds he studied the motionless shape in the center of the bed. Then his arm straightened as he took aim, and the gun spoke twice, softly.

The chuffing coughs were apologetic in the hushed

confines of the room. A few seconds later he fired again, the shot slightly louder. The barrel rose with each explosion as overheated gasses kicked back against the gunman's hand. Runner saw the muscle in the side of his face jerk each time it happened.

The hollow-nosed bullets tore through the dummy, through Olana's clothing, ruining hundreds if not thousands of dollars in an instant. It continued on, through the mattress beneath and the box spring. The second bullet touched one of the metal coils and was deflected straight down into the floor, tearing through a ceiling fixture in the room below. Wires shorted as they were cut; the heat of the short circuit was enough to start one hundred sixty-year-old wood shavings to burning around the hole that had been cut through the ceiling to accept the wiring.

The first bullet did no damage, except aesthetic, as it hit the thick shag carpet of Olana Venedris' bedroom at an angle that sent it plowing a ferule between floor and rug, scarring flooring that had been laid down during the administration of James Madison. The third bullet tore at a much shallower angle, through mattress and box spring to chunk solidly into the headboard of the bed.

Someone was in the room below. Runner heard a muffled scream as he rabbit-punched the assassin; the bedroom was not as soundproofed as he had thought.

The man dropped, paralyzed by the first blow. He landed on his face, smashing his nose. The gun flew from his hand as he hit the floor.

Runner chased the gun and caught it by the silencer, cursing aloud as he threw it away again with his burned hand. He clenched the injured palm, tears starting in his eyes, while the automatic bounced halfway across the room and slid beneath a vanity table.

Runner retrieved the gun, careful to pick it up by the grip, then dropped it on the vanity long enough to smear cream from one of Olana's jars across the burn. Then he brought the automatic back to the bed where he used one of the drapery panels to unscrew the overheated silencer. Never fire a silenced gun rapidly. The expanding gasses made the noise; the principle of the gadget was to trap those gasses, preventing the noise by keeping them prisoner.

After one shot the silencer was hot. After three its useful life had been ended. Now it was nothing more than fifty dollars or so of junk.

The idiot on the floor was lucky the gun hadn't blown up in his face on the second shot. He'd exhausted this year's ration of luck by firing it the third time.

There seemed little point in remaining in darkness after the uproar going on in the room below. Runner turned on the nearest lamp. It wouldn't be long before someone came up to see why the assassin hadn't reported his success.

He examined the gun: a .9 millimeter copy of Browning's design. The manufacturer's name was stamped into the steel beneath the copy's action: Aramco.

Runner released the clip. It held eight shots.

The man on the floor had shot three times. Assuming the clip was full when he started, five were left.

He turned the man over with his foot; he was a stranger.

Runner spared the assassin ten seconds to search his pockets, flipping the wallet open to read the name on the driver's license: Fred Faxler. Twenty-two years old, if the license wasn't a phony. His features were battered, coarsened. A street punk. Hired muscle.

He certainly didn't belong in this house.

Runner tossed the wallet back onto the man's chest as he straightened; he hadn't bothered to count the money. He headed for the door. It opened while he was still five paces away.

Another stranger stood there.

"What the—"

The newcomer swallowed the obscenity as his eyes moved from Runner to the man on the floor. Runner stopped, the captured weapon still in his hand. Only then did the man reached for the revolver thrust into his belt.

Runner shot him.

He fired once; it was enough. The impact of the hollow-nosed bullet from the large caliber automatic threw the man back, his own weapon flying from his hand. He hit the doorjamb like a limp rag, all tension concentrated on the tremendous ache in his guts where Runner's bullet had turned his intestines to hamburger. His spine, and then the back of his skull, struck the wood frame; his right hand slapped against the wall, shattering a small oval antique mirror hanging there, but he wasn't concerned about seven years' bad luck. His left hand swung wildly through the open doorway. Momentum carried him completely around, his spine glued to the jamb. Runner heard the left hand slap the wall in the hall before the man fell, splinters from the doorjamb ripping his shirt and stabbing deep into his butt.

He never felt them: splinters, or the pain of hitting so

hard. He was dead, his heart exploded by the expanding force of the bullet in his guts.

Runner scooped up the revolver, tucking it into his hip pocket; he never carried a billfold. He stepped across the body, which was already stinking with released body wastes, and moved into the hall.

Two down: the two strangers.

The stairs rose from second floor front to third floor rear. Runner was halfway there when he heard the pounding of heavy feet. Ramsey's two hundred seventy pounds shook the framing of the house as the black took the lower flight two steps at a time, then made the turn and started toward the third floor.

Runner had reached the railing circling the stairwell. Ramsey looked up, saw him before he could duck away. The gun in the black's hand looked like a toy, almost swallowed in his fist; his finger was almost too large to fit through the trigger guard.

Runner fired: the gun didn't.

Ramsey grinned, started up again. Runner wasted no time trying to make the damned thing work—he threw the automatic at the black.

Ramsey ducked to one side, arm over his face. Runner didn't bother with the revolver he had taken from the second man. He vaulted over the railing, dropped with stiff legs onto the black.

He hit with his heels, smashing the giant's collarbone—nearly breaking the tarsals and metatarsals in his right foot. Ramsey slammed around, against the wall, stunned and paralyzed in his right arm.

Runner fell onto the stairs, hitting hard; he saw red and sucked in breath against the double shock to his system. Ramsey's hand holding the gun hung useless. The black pushed away from the wall with his other hand, anger a low growl in his throat as he swung wildly while Runner rolled away. He came up to slam his shoulder into the giant's gut, throwing him back again. Before the black could move, Runner grabbed the paralyzed arm, applied a come-along to the fingers with his full strength.

Ramsey screamed in agony as his fingers were doubled; the edge of the metacarpals shattered and splintered under the pressure. Runner yanked down on the hand, then grabbed the underside of the arm and used it as a lever to swing the black around. He crashed through the stair balustrade and went over, down onto the first flight. Runner released his grip before he went flying after him, and Ramsey tumbled limply down half the flight before coming to a rest with his head at a peculiar angle.

"Dr. Runner!"

Runner looked up. A white-haired woman dressed in a long flannel nightgown stood in the door of the room below Olana's. She clutched her right fist to her chest.

"Who are you?"

"Uh . . . Agatha. Agatha Twilty." She stared wide-eyed. "What is happening?"

Twilty's telephone voice was thirty years younger than her body; Runner knew brief disappointment. The secretary was one scream from total panic.

"It's all right, Miss Twilty. Just a small problem."

Runner could smell the stink of scorched wiring as Agatha Twilty closed her eyes and sank to a sitting position against the wall. He knew instinctively that she had no part in this affair.

He stepped across several smashed banisters, spared a single glance into the bedroom. The ceiling fixture hung by a wire; Agatha had dragged a chair over beneath it, standing there to use the fire extinguisher that now lay abandoned. Foam from the extinguisher filled the hole in the ceiling, dripping down the fixture and over the chair and the carpet, but the fire danger was over.

Runner smiled at the woman. She had practically dealt with the emergency of the moment before giving in to panic. He decided he liked Agatha.

He moved down the stairs, bent to check Ramsey. The black's neck had broken in the fall, but he was still breathing. He'd be all right if he didn't try to move before the paramedics arrived.

Three down.

Four, counting Agatha.

That left Olana.

Even as Runner formed the thought, he knew the woman had fled.

He came down the rest of the stairs. The library doors stood wide; he moved in quickly and found his shoes, still under the coffee table where abandoned. His tie was across the arm of the sofa; someone had hung his jacket carefully over the back of a chair.

Runner slipped into his shoes, gave a quick search of the rest of the house. The kitchen opened onto a tiny garden; a gate in the back wall swung loose. Olana had come this way. He knew she had no intention of returning, at least for the present.

He went back into the house, checked Ramsey again; then he picked up Agatha Twilty and carried her into her bedroom. She was chunky, at least thirty pounds overweight. He grunted when he dropped her onto the bed, and her eyes flew open.

"Oh!" Runner drew up the covers. "Dr. Runner!"

"You'll be all right, Miss Twilty. Rest a few minutes. I'm going now, but ten minutes after I leave you should call an ambulance for Ramsey. And for the two men upstairs."

"Two men?" She shook her head, confused. "Doctor, what is *happening*?"

"Ask Madame Olana when she returns."

Runner turned away as he said the last, and the woman wailed behind him: "But where is she? *Doctor!*"

He waved at her as he left the room, hurrying downstairs to the library to reclaim his jacket; he stuffed the tie in his pocket. A closet beneath the stairs proved to hold his outerwear.

Runner started to leave the house; then he turned back. Now that the danger was dealt with, his mind shifted back into gear. He could think rationally again.

Olana was involved in the murders.

Her actions last night and this morning proved the point: She had arranged a trap for Runner. Ergo, she knew he was deep in the investigation. Perhaps she had even arranged the deaths of the agents. If the latter, she certainly knew he was supposed to be the patsy for Sandra Blake. How had she received her information?

Someone had told her.

There was no longer immediate danger in this house, but Runner's warning system told him it would be foolish to stay any longer. Still, he moved to the desk, quickly going through the papers on the top.

It was all innocuous: charts in progress for clients,

none of whom were named. Penciled codes at the top of each sheet identified the subject to the astrologer.

Was another agent among these?

It didn't matter; certainly they wouldn't try the same method again, now that they had been discovered.

He opened the shallow drawer, found it filled with the usual junk of desks: pencils, clips, rubber bands, ink pads. A memo pad was imprinted at the top with zodiacal symbols; the top sheet bore the sign for Sagittarius and PM, the R=C, 817 scrawled boldly underneath.

Runner studied the figures for nearly a minute, then reached for the ornate French cradle telephone. He dialed the number of The Ritz-Carlton, waited for eleven rings before the operator responded.

"This is Doctor Runner, in 612. Are there any messages for me?"

"One moment, please." She came back. "Yes, Mr. Monaghan has been trying to reach you all evening. He left word you're to come to his room the moment you return."

"What room number?"

"Eight hundred seventeen, doctor."

Several seconds passed before he remembered to say "Thank you," and hung up. He stood behind the table a moment longer, all ten fingertips resting against the surface.

Phil Monaghan was the informant.

NINE

Hatred welled in Runner's gut, grew like an expanding cloud until it exploded into a firebomb that sent him into an unreasoning rage. His eyes closed tight, jaws clenched; a low growl started deep in his chest, rose through his throat to become a scream:

"Arrggghhhhh!"

"Doctor Runner!"

He opened his eyes, staring wildly; his hands were beneath the table, ready to throw it over.

Runner sucked in breath, let it out again raggedly. Agatha Twilty stood in the library doorway, her hand clutching the top of the sensible robe she had donned. She'd done something to her hair as well, but fright was evident on her face.

"Are you all right, doctor?"

He swallowed before answering, breathed in again and let the air trickle from his lungs as he commanded his heartbeat to slow. His chest rose and fell slowly; there was pain in his gut.

Runner glanced down. His fingers had twisted and

crumpled the papers on the desk, tearing a half-inch sheaf almost through.

"I'm . . . yes, Miss Twilty. I'm all right."

The emotion storm ebbed. His vision cleared of the red haze of anger, although the hatred was still there, a physical presence in his gut.

"Thank goodness!" said the elderly secretary. "You frightened me, doctor. I thought you were going to smash something."

"I'm sorry. Forgive me."

A berserk rage had come upon him again. What was happening to him?

Monaghan . . . the first emotional storm subsided. He knew he had leaped to a conclusion about the Irish agent upon no more evidence than the scribbled note in Olana Venedris' desk. Flimsy enough to convict the man, particularly when he realized his own dislike of Monaghan colored his feelings. They'd been antagonists ten years ago and now the man was back to tear apart his life again.

Hatred . . . the emotion was strong. In the past Monaghan had been an annoyance. No more. He could remember no such strong an emotional reaction to anyone, to anything— until the loss of the patrol.

A robot? Once, perhaps.

That was over now. He was involved in the world, with people. The robot had been touched with emotion; Runner knew he would never be dispassionate about people, about events, again.

"I thought you were going to stay in bed?"

Agatha Twilty seemed to gather herself together; she shook her head, firmly.

"No. I . . . behaved foolishly. I'm a sensible person, Doctor Runner, and I am now in control of myself. I expected . . . something of the sort. Of what happened.''

"Well, I'm sure everything will work out, Miss Twilty. Right now I have to leave.

"I must talk to you first."

"Really, I can't spare the time."

"Are you aware the house is being watched?"

He blinked. "Are you certain?"

"Two men are out in front. I saw them from my bedroom window. I don't know either of them."

"Did they see you?"

"No. At least, I don't think so," she amended. "I had turned my light off, was coming downstairs to catch you before you left. I wanted to see if the sun had come up."

Runner glanced at his watch: a few minutes before seven. Barely twenty minutes ago he had awakened in Olana Venedris' bed.

He had seen no one watching the house when he checked her windows. If they were her men, they should have been inside, reinforcements for the gunmen.

Monaghan's men?

"Doctor, I'm going to make a pot of tea," said Agatha. "Please, don't leave. What I have to say is very important . . . you will want to hear it."

Runner saw that she was still quite agitated beneath her manner of calm. He followed her back into the kitchen, dropping onto a stool while she started fire under the kettle and measured loose tea into an incongruously cheerful yellow pot.

"Will you take tea, doctor?"

He shrugged. "Thank you, yes."

Agatha's hands trembled as she produced cups, saucers, spoons, creamer, sugar bowl. He could see her teeth working against her lower lip as she measured everything out carefully, stalling until the water boiled. Only when the tea was steeping in the pot did she sit down herself and fold her hands on the edge of the worktable.

"Doctor, do you know Senator Wendell Tucker? Are you familiar with the senator?" she corrected.

Runner shrugged. Even ignoring the daily newscasts and the daily newspapers, he could not completely escape the media exploitation of the country's favorite public people. Tucker was being touted as the man on a white horse who would be the savior of the Republican party in the next national elections. Or the Democrats; he wasn't sure which.

Whichever, the presidential nomination was Tucker's for the asking. Personally charming, he was popu- with his constituents and with the Capitol Press Corps. He played the talk-show circuit, the knight in shining armor who could show America the way into the future.

The senator had written a book; all aspirants to the top political office had to write a book. Somebody had given a copy to Runner: *The Center of the Road: American's Turnpike to the Future*. He had flipped through the opening chapters. Glibly written, probably by a professional ghostwriter, it was a distillation of the social theories of the liberal Left and the economic theories of the conservative Right. Its publication had been a media event: a Book of the Month Club Main Selection and rising to Number Two on the best-seller lists.

"My daughter, Carla, is Senator Tucker's special assistant," said Agatha.

Runner raised an eyebrow, and she continued: "The senator is a wonderful man. Carla has been with him more than ten years, since he first ran for Congress. She worships him, doctor, and I must tell you I think she is right to do so. She was right."

Agatha warmed to her subject. She poured the tea into their cups without a pause in her flow of words, except to take a single sip.

"Wendell Tucker will be the president we've needed for the past fifty years, doctor. The best in this century . . . if he can be removed from the evil influence of Olana Venedris."

"What influence, Miss Twilty? And in what way does this involve me?"

"I don't know," she admitted, answering the last part of his question. "I'm not sure. Hear me out, please."

Agatha told her story. Two years ago, shortly after the publication of his book, Wendell Tucker had been introduced to Olana at a Washington cocktail party.

The astrologer's reputation was already established, her star in the ascendant. The fact that she was also beautiful served as a magnet to the senator, whose romantic life was straitjacketed by the long illness of his wife. Olana deliberately struck sexual sparks, arranged a consultation by promising to chart his horoscope.

The senator was amused by the thought; he had been a notorious skeptic as to the occult. Until he returned from his first liaison with the gypsy woman. It was only the first; he began to invent excuses to fly to Boston, to New York, to wherever Olana might be.

"It's an old story, of course," said Agatha, primly, showing her disapproval of Tucker's weakness of the flesh. "But understandable. His wife died last year and ever since he has been completely dependent on her—Olana."

There was a bad taste in her mouth when she said the name. "Olana Venedris is an evil woman," she added, a moment later, reiterating her earlier statement. "Would you like to know what she said, when I told her yesterday you were coming?"

"What?" he asked, fascinated.

" ' "Oh spider, dear spider!" cried the stupid little fly. "Please let me come into your parlor, oh magnificent spider, that I may die!" ' "

She sighed, and shook her head. "Doctor, I came to this house about six months ago, hoping I could find out just what she is planning for Senator Tucker. I was personal secretary to the head of a very large corporation, worked for him for thirty years. When he retired, the company let me retire as well.

"Olana's secretary left her about the same time," she continued. "She is a very difficult person to work for. Carla was already concerned for the senator and she arranged for me to have the job. I am very good at my work. Olana relies on me in almost everything. I'm supposed to take the shuttle to New York this afternoon and join her there."

"She planned leaving today?" asked Runner.

"Oh, yes. Olana spends more time in New York than in Boston, at least since I've been with her. "I've watched her," she said, after sipping again at her tea. "I've seen what she does to people. Heard what she tells those who come to her for advice. She is evil, doctor. Make no mistake about that."

"What is it you expect of me?" he asked, when Agatha was silent for nearly a minute.

"I don't know," she admitted. "I don't know why she is . . . against you. She is your enemy, implacably so. I think she will stop at nothing."

There was nothing to say to that. He wondered if Agatha realized Olana had planned to have him killed?

"Could you approach the senator?" she asked. "Carla could set up an appointment for you. I don't know what good it would do, but we have to do *something*."

Runner considered the suggestion. He was deeply involved in this matter, thanks to whoever had planned the death of Sandra Blake. Monaghan had given him a chance to clear himself—if the agent didn't have some deeper motive. If he weren't in collusion with the astrologer.

"Let's go back to the library," he said. "I have something I want you to see."

Agatha examined the memo pad and shrugged. "PM. The Ritz-Carlton. I suppose it refers to the afternoon or the evening. It is Olana's handwriting."

"Does the name Monaghan mean anything?"

Agatha furrowed her brow. "I knew a Joe Monaghan once." The prim Miss Twilty blushed and looked down at her hands. "He was a salesman. A very persistent sort. Joe thought he was God's gift to the ladies." She looked up again. "But lord, that was thirty years ago or more."

Agatha didn't know Monaghan. Which meant nothing . . . or something. Runner wasn't sure.

But now that his rage had subsided, he could think dispassionately about the Irish agent. The memo pad was damning, but certainly not proof. If Olana knew that Runner was on the other side, she could as easily know about Monaghan's role.

The Irishman had brought Runner into the investigation; he shouldn't lose track of that fact. Would Monaghan now be working both ends of the street: a mole?

The agent was Runner's only contact with the supposed Special Group; the others he had seen were only clerks, couriers, civil-service types. Their like could be found in any large organization. And these days the underworld was as well organized as legitimate business.

There were supposedly Mafia connections to Monaghan's conspiracy, if the dark plot did exist. That could explain Olana's muscle, although it did not explain the astrologer's role in what was happening.

Runner knew he needed a way to cross-check Monaghan's credentials. He closed his eyes, spun the rolodex file in his memory. It stopped at a name from Korea: Vic Bremmer. Bremmer was a sergeant in Runner's platoon; for a time they had been close. After his tour of duty, Bremmer was recruited by the CIA.

Runner had run into him two or three years ago, during a student demonstration against CIA recruitment on campus. Bremmer was there to soothe the ruffled feathers of the administration; he admitted to Runner that he spent most of his time nowadays acting in such liaisons.

The two former comrades-in-arms spent ten minutes exchanging reminiscences of their youth and phone numbers. They promised to get together someday soon, although Bremmer had no more desire to do so than Runner.

The number was in McLean, Virginia. Runner dialed the ridiculous telephone; the phone was picked up in the middle of the fourth ring. Bremmer's voice sounded sleepy and disgruntled.

"Jesus, man! It's the crack of dawn!"

Runner identified himself and apologized for the early call. After a minute he heard a querulous voice in the background, and then a giggle, followed by the sharp crack of a hand against bare flesh. The giggler let out an outraged squeal.

"Simmer down! Yeah, James. Excuse me." Bremmer yawned widely. "Jesus, I hate mornings! You didn't call me to chat, so what's up?"

Runner told him; Bremmer was silent during the explanation, then came back with: "Monaghan. Redhead, big burly guy. Michael O'Shea type."

"I don't know who O'Shea might be," said Runner. "But yes, you have him."

"Met him once or twice. We didn't gel. The son-of-a-bitch tried to throw his weight around. Looking out for number one, out for the main chance, that type."

"That's Monaghan," said Runner, dryly.

"He's legit—he is in the community, James. As to the Special Group, I don't know it, but that means nothing. The president could have a thousand special groups going and only the Deputy Director and the men actually involved would know. But I'll check it out. Who's the man who's supposed to be ours?"

Runner was forced to admit he didn't know. He could visualize Bremmer's head shake.

"I'll check it out," said Bremmer again. "Where can I reach you?"

"I'll call you this afternoon."

"Fine. After three."

Bremmer gave his office number and hung up. Runner's doubts had not been lifted. Would not be lifted until the agent was given a clear bill of health by people Runner respected and believed, or by developments.

He was supposed to check in with Monaghan now. Runner had already rejected that course of action.

What to do?

He had already made up his mind: follow Olana. She was definitely on the other side. And at the moment she was his only lead to the men responsible for Sandy's death.

Ramsey screamed. The hackles on Runner's neck shot up straight and Agatha took a single step backward and cracked herself in the teeth as she raised her hand to cover her mouth.

The cry was one of agony; it cut off short in a gurgle. Runner moved, heading for the door, and stopped short as he saw the man who had come into Olana's bedroom to kill him.

The assassin had come three steps down the stairs; he carried another gun. Ramsey's.

He fired three times while Runner tried to throw his topcoat and jacket out of the way to reach the revolver in his hip pocket. The gun's sight snagged on the band of the pocket while bullets chunked into the wall and into the door only inches from Runner's ear.

He ducked back, but the killer realized the distance was too great for accuracy. The shooting stopped as the man retreated to the second floor. Runner heard his footsteps diminishing; they vanished.

"Is there another way down?" he demanded, wheeling on Agatha.

"The back stairs," she gasped. "They come out in the pantry. Please, doctor, be careful!"

The last was wasted; Runner was already halfway to the kitchen. He burst through in time to see the killer leap from the back stoop.

Runner straight-armed the closing storm door, landed six feet into the garden; his ankle twisted painfully as he came down on a circle of painted cobblestones. He limped on, into the alley, in time to see the killer dragging his own leg. The man turned and snapped off another shot that went wild, ricocheting overhead; Runner heard glass break. Somebody just had an unpleasant awakening.

The killer fired again; the gun didn't. Olana supplied lousy armament for her troops. He threw the gun away, angry, and turned to do battle with the outer gate as Runner began sprinting again, ignoring the pain in his ankle. He was almost to the man as the gate swung open; the killer moved into the street—

A rifle cracked once; in the cold morning air it sounded like a stick breaking. The small gun had seemed much louder in the house and in the alley.

The killer stopped as though he had run into a brick wall. For an instant he hung there, Runner holding the gate behind him, then he fell into the street.

"Hey!"

Runner felt foolish even as he shouted; the rifle answered, splintering the top of the gate.

He ducked back, heart pounding wildly. The muzzle

flare came from behind a car across the street. It was light enough now that the rifleman had had a clear look at him before shooting.

Olana's muscle was eliminated.

The same people tried to take out Runner.

It didn't make sense. Unless there was a third party involved he didn't know anything about.

He retreated to the garden, waited there a moment to be sure the ambushers weren't coming after him. No one appeared to disturb the gate.

Runner turned, scanned the garden. Eight-foot brick walls blocked out the intruding apartment buildings on either side, but there was a gap between them.

Assume the men in front were part of the same team as the men in back. He couldn't walk out the front door. Nor could he use the alley.

A rusted wheelbarrow was turned up against one wall. He used it as a step to climb the wall, hooking his arm over the top. The next building was only about three feet away, but a spiked-top iron fence sprouted half-way between, protecting the apartments from the snobs in the house. The spikes came within six inches of the top of the brick wall. The ground on this side of the fence was rough, strewn with rubble and trash. On the other side was a concrete gutter carrying stagnant water and more trash. The gutter had a lip less than two inches wide on either side.

To the rear, the little passage was completely blocked. If he went out the front, he would be in plain sight of the waiting men.

The apartment building had windows in this wall, even though the tenants on the first four floors had a view only of the town house. There were windows in the house as well, but they were shuttered over.

Runner scanned the windows: one gave onto a cross-corridor, a casement that turned out on a crank. He pulled himself the rest of the way on to the wall, brought out a glove and leaned against the second floor window. The glove went over the glass; the butt of the revolver cracked it once, and then a second time, pushing the leather through the hole he made.

He pulled the glove onto his hand, reached through; he could just operate the crank with the tips of his fingers. Satisfied, he dropped back into the garden and returned to the house.

Agatha waited in the hall, wringing her hands nervously. She sighed when she saw he was unharmed.

"Ramsey is dead."

Runner accepted the statement. "What was his place here?"

"Houseman, chauffeur. Not that he did much of either," she added with a sniff. "I think he was her bodyguard. Olana never went any place without him." Then she added, "I looked at the other man upstairs. I've never seen him before."

"Hired muscle," said Runner. "Agatha . . . Miss Twilty. I'm going to New York. Where can I find Olana?"

"There's an estate in Westchester County. Near Pound Ridge." She gave him the address, told Runner how to find the place. "It belongs to one of her clients, but she has had the use of it ever since I've worked for her."

With all the shooting, Runner couldn't understand why the police hadn't showed in force. Unless the men outside were official.

Even as he formed the thought, he was sure they were.

Reinforcements, brought in by Monaghan?

He didn't let his doubts assail him. Someone had marked him as a target; it didn't matter who, so long as he was in the line of fire.

He had to get away from Boston, but he didn't dare try for his car. If Monaghan were behind this, the hotel and its garage would be watched.

"What shuttle will you take?"

"It doesn't make much difference," Agatha said. "I take whatever is convenient."

"Let's go up to your room. I want to see where the men you spotted are placed."

Agatha moved well for a woman of her bulk. Runner followed her to the bedroom, peered through a one-inch gap in the drapes after she pointed out the plants.

One waited at the corner, moving around in the cold, as though waiting for a late ride. The other was in a car illegally parked by the fire hydrant. The man on the corner kept on dancing, but he never turned away from line of sight of the house for more than three seconds.

There were others on the street now, half-a-dozen men and women coming from the apartment buildings, heading for work. Most of them aimed for Columbus; that was good. They provided a screen.

"Get dressed. Please," he added. "And call a cab. Do you have a bag packed?"

"I'm always packed," said Agatha. "I never know when Olana is going to pick up for Washington or San Francisco, or lord knows where."

"Order the cab for Logan. We'll change the destination when we're in it to one of the downtown car rental offices. I want you to rent me a car.''

Perhaps he was being overly cautious, laying a false trail this way. There was no reason to suspect Monaghan, or Olana, or whoever, of covering the cab companies, the airport, the terminals.

But caution cost nothing extra. And every fiber of his being was on the alert.

Runner waited for Agatha to finish dressing, too keyed up to do anything but pace the library. After a minute he tried the cabinet, but found nothing revealing of the astrologer's background, or backing. There was no time to search for her files.

Agatha came down, prim and matronly; Runner had already placed her bag by the front door. She ordered the cab—and he took a deep breath, then returned to the garden.

It was time to go over the wall, enter where he had already broken.

TEN

Runner used the same wheelbarrow to vault onto the top of the wall, and pulled himself precariously to his feet. He had difficulty maintaining balance on the leather soles of his shoes.

He leaned across the gap, supporting himself on his stiff left arm while he put his right hand through the hole in the window—and yanked it back.

A young woman came out of an apartment, turned away to fumble her key from her purse; she was dressed for the street. She locked both latch and deadbolt. Preoccupied, she hadn't seen the man at the window.

As he dropped flat to the top of the wall, Runner winced against pain. A shard of glass had ripped across the surface of his glove, cutting through almost to the back of his hand. He peeled down the glove, saw a white scratch; but there was no blood.

The wall wasn't wide enough. Runner hung over several inches on either side, and one shoe toe slipped free, banging his knee cap. He sucked in a sharp breath against the new pain, damning the slippery leather.

But he hadn't expected to be scaling walls.

Or to be the target of opposing sides in a gun battle.

Face turned against his arm, Runner breathed slowly while he counted off sixty seconds. His heart was beating more rapidly as adrenalin again surged through his system. From the top of the wall he looked down the narrow slit between house and apartment building, saw a cab pass by, coming from Columbus.

The one summoned by Agatha?

If it were, Runner trusted Agatha Twilty to stall the driver until he made it into the other building. More disturbing, it was light enough now that anyone looking between the buildings would have to see him.

And at that instant someone appeared: a man. He didn't glance toward Runner as he disappeared.

Runner realized he was holding his breath. He let it out and carefully pulled himself erect, cataloguing several new pains.

The woman had gone.

Three other apartments opened off the corridor. Two had morning papers lying in front of the doors. Hoping the tenants were late risers, Runner let the shard that had done the damage to his hand drop into the gutter. The piece of glass bounced off a chunk of broken concrete, shattering. To his heightened hearing, it sounded like an explosion.

Traffic on Holden was growing heavier; he heard a car engine roar as it was started, revved up to prevent it from stalling. Another car passed by and seconds later, a panel truck. Time was running out.

He tried the hole again; this time his hand passed through easily and his fingertips caught the handle of the crank. Runner twisted his hand around inside the window, doubled it over as he strained to operate the stubborn crank.

The mechanism refused to work; the window resisted, stuck to its weather stripping as though glued. He tried again, afraid he was going to have to break out more of the glass, and it gave, suddenly and with a noisy creak.

The casement panel swung out, paused as Runner nearly lost his balance. He scrabbled wildly, at last locked his heel against the edge of the wall. He carefully raised back to vertical, aware of the spikes too near below. Fall, and he'd be impaled on the iron fence.

Perspiration soaked his forehead and his armpits as he recovered; but now he could reach through the opening, operate the crank easily. The panel swung out into open position; at vertical to the frame, there was a three inch gap on the wall side, no more than nine or ten inches on the other.

It wasn't enough. Runner eyed the narrow opening, considered retreating. But now he had come this far he didn't want to backtrack.

He stepped across the gap, slipped one foot through the opening . . . he was stuck on his clothing. He stepped down with his outside foot to the top of the spiked fence and wriggled out of his coats, tossing them through the open window. Then he sucked in his gut and pulled himself into the slot again.

The window was tall enough to take most of his height; he was forced to bend his knees only slightly as he slipped his hips through the space. But his chest was another matter. The panel shifted against his back as he first took in air, then emptied his lungs completely.

The fit was still too tight. He fought the opening,

tried to retreat a bit. Fabric ripped: his shirt had torn. He arched his back, cracked his head against the glass—banged his forehead against the center post in reaction.

Runner tried again. The iron frame creaked dangerously, metal snapped and the panel swung free of the crank.

He was through.

He dropped down from the windowsill and scooped up his coats, took a few precious seconds to press the panel back into its frame. The break would be discovered the first time someone came this way. Maybe the building would improve its security.

Another corridor cut through the building from front to rear: an elevator was at the back, fire stairs beside it. Runner slipped into the coats and took the stairs three at a time, pausing again to ease the door open far enough to check the outer lobby.

The elevator started in the shaft beside him. He jumped. The car headed up, summoned to the top floor.

The lobby was empty. He moved out of the stairs, came far enough toward the foyer to see the man on the far corner. His attention was completely on the house, not on the neighboring buildings.

Runner slipped into the foyer. He couldn't see the stoop of the house, but the cab had U-turned, waited outside the gate. The door of the cab opened and the driver got out, taking Agatha's bag from her hand as she came through the gate.

Agatha must have watched Runner's progress from the back of the house, perhaps the kitchen, waiting until she saw he was safely through before coming out.

The driver got back into the cab after closing the rear

door for Agatha. The car swung away from the curb—swung back in again in front of the apartment building, just as the elevator stopped on the first floor.

Runner glanced over his shoulder as he pushed through the outside door. A middle-aged man came out of the elevator, stopped in surprise as he saw Runner.

Agatha had the door of the cab open as Runner came out of the building, fast. Hunched low, he saw the man on the corner open his mouth to shout. He was in the back seat before the gun came out of the man's pocket, too late.

He twisted, stared through the back window. The other man was climbing out of the car.

"Logan, right?" asked the cabbie, glancing at Runner in his rearview mirror. If he thought anything strange was happening, he kept his opinion to himself.

"No. Downtown," said Runner, settling. "Hertz, or Avis—whichever of the car rental companies is easiest to reach. And is open this early."

"You'll do better at the airport," said the driver. "Most of the downtown agencies don't open until eight. They operate twenty-four hours at Logan."

"All right," said Runner. "The airport. But make it fast."

The driver had spotted the gun in the hand of the man on the corner. He was already on Columbus, heading the wrong way. He made a sharp right, leaving rubber, and cut over to the next main street, then turned right again. Half a mile later he cut back over to Columbus.

Traffic was growing into the morning rush. The taxi left the surface streets at the Massachusetts Turnpike, then made the swing onto Ninety-three and into the Fitzgerald Expressway. From there it was a short run through the Callahan Tunnel; Runner handed the toll over the seat, envying the outbound traffic as it flowed unimpeded.

Agatha scrutinized Runner, shook her head ruefully. "Your clothes are a mess. I have a comb in my pocket if you'd like to use it."

Runner twisted around to see the top of his head in the rearview mirror, then accepted the comb, making what repairs he could. He tucked his torn shirt back into his trousers. No wonder the man coming out of the elevator had stopped to stare.

As the driver braked the cab before the Hertz agency, Runner handed him a twenty.

"You dropped us at the terminals."

The cabbie had listened with one ear to the disjointed conversation of his passengers, had heard Agatha call Runner Doctor.

"Sure thing, doc. Any in particular?"

"Eastern. The shuttle."

Runner made the decision even as the question was asked; the cabbie nodded. The twenty disappeared, and he got out to open the door, but Runner beat him to it.

Whoever was after him, they'd guess he headed out of town when he didn't report in to Monaghan. If Monaghan was involved.

New York was a logical destination, since Olana's main base of operations was there. He didn't worry about evading them there. He'd have the advantage of a different form of transportation than they expected.

"Buy two tickets," he said. "One in my name."

"Sometimes I buy my ticket on the plane," said Agatha.

"Get these at the counter. Wait a flight, if necessary."

She nodded as he carried her bag into the agency. There Runner fretted while Agatha went through the details of filling out the rental agreement, acceded to full insurance coverage. The male clerk seemed emotionally distraught to learn there was no reservation. He forced them to wait an extra five minutes before coming back to say he had managed to find them a car.

Agatha was ready to explode, thereby saving Runner the trouble, before the keys and a copy of the rental agreement were finally in her hands. She gave the keys to Runner and he drove her to Eastern's terminal.

"Doctor, promise me you'll contact Carla," she begged, before getting out of the car. "She may be able to help you. At least she can put you in touch with other people in Washington."

Runner made the promise and Agatha left. Her head was held high as she marched into the terminal, her plump legs pumping forcefully.

He smiled; he liked Agatha Twilty.

Too bad she wasn't thirty years younger. Twenty.

Runner headed the car south, through the tunnel again, and back onto Ninety-five. Although logic told him he was clear of the men at the astrologer's house, tension didn't ebb until he cleared the city limits.

New York was two hundred twenty-five miles away.

*   *   *

The drive gave Runner time to think. He kept the car to a careful fifty-five, resisting the urge to move out with the traffic that passed him, sometimes on both sides. It was twenty minutes before he got the feel of the Cutlass, before it stopped wallowing. He missed the Mercedes. No wonder Americans were the softest people in the world.

He pulled into the first service area, ravenously hungry now that the tension of the escape had eased. The waitress was flustered by his order for five scrambled eggs, two ham steaks, a twelve ounce tumbler of orange juice, a double order of toast, a side of fresh tomatoes. She was forced to summon the manager to figure out the amount to place on the check.

In normal times that amount of food would have left him sluggish, if he could down it at all. Now it served to satisfy his inner engine as he returned to the car, started south again.

Monaghan. Runner's thinking processes returned to logic, rejected passion. He'd always considered the Irishman an opportunist, amoral, concerned only with what was best for Phil Monaghan. An army careerist because it was respectable, and because he'd balanced the risks of going into the rackets along with most of his boyhood friends and found them wanting. Monaghan was a glory seeker, trying to build a reputation, using his army contacts to further his civilian ambitions. Not above illicit activity when the risks were minimal, and not above turning in his illicit companions when the reward for doing so was greater than the profits to be earned from breaking the rules.

Monaghan could become a double agent, if the payoff was large enough to balance the risks. Yet Runner couldn't convict him on evidence as flimsy as scribbled notes on Olana's memo pad.

The situation was complicated. It would be nice to know Monaghan was no more than he pretended to be.

On the other hand, it would be best to know if he had turned around, switched his loyalties.

Runner's spine crawled, as though someone was watching him. He didn't like the sensation.

At the legal speed limit, it was past noon before he crossed the New York State line, headed down the Bruckner Expressway and across the Triboro, then down the F. D. R. Drive. He left the expressway at 86th Street, turned down York Avenue.

He needed a place to come to ground. Runner had one old friend in New York City, an occultist who operated an occult bookstore in Yorkville. He found a public garage on 82nd Street and surrendered the keys for a receipt, then walked back up three blocks, turned east.

The Talisman was one of hundreds of such shops throughout Yorkville, a dusty, cluttered street-front affair crammed between a shop that sold kites and a natural food sandwich shop. A yellowed placard with a clock's face said: Back at 1:00. It was 1:15.

Runner pressed the doorbell; nothing happened. He stepped onto the sidewalk far enough to see the second floor window; it bore the same gold script lettering as the main show window and was filled with the same stacks of books. That was new; Wilhelm Forrest always kept that window clear, usually opened two inches no matter the time of year or the weather.

He should have phoned; Runner looked toward the corner, spotted a phone booth. When he reached it, a yellow out-of-order sticker was plastered across the coin slot. Unnecessarily. The cable had been ripped from the receiver, which lay smashed on the floor, almost buried by rubble.

Frustrated by the realities of returning to New York, Runner moved away from the booth just as a little white-haired old man came bustling around the corner, his arms burdened by the single bag of groceries he carried. He pushed past, puffing.

"Wilhelm! Willy Forrest!"

The old man stopped, peered myopically around; his face broadened into a smile.

"James! Dear boy! What a delightful surprise!"

Willy Forrest bubbled as Runner took the groceries from him, almost bouncing as his little legs stretched to keep up with the younger man. He was no more than five feet tall, the sweeping mustachios swirling across his face almost making him top-heavy. He was rotund, roly-poly; add a full beard, and he could be costumed as the perfect Saint Nick.

"Why didn't you call, James, warn an old man you were coming?" Willy fumbled in his pocket for keys, produced a tangle of big red bandanna, ticket stubs, receipts, before coming up with the ring. "Come in, come in!"

The bookshop was a single long, narrow room, dusty and lined with floor-to-ceiling shelves from front to back. Runner sneezed as dust swirled into his nostrils. A row of tables ran down the center of the store, leaving bare space for owner and customers to maneuver through the aisles. A high short counter at the front held an ancient mechanical cash register and more untidy stacks of books.

"You should always call, James," said Willy, firmly as he pulled the clock card from the door and thrust in another that said Closed. "I would have fixed my *stufato* for you and bought some of Beck's marvelous *strudel*, from up the Avenue."

Runner leaned back against a table, pushing over a pile of books, as the tiny proprietor squeezed by. He followed Willy through the shop and up narrow stairs to the railroad flat that served as adjunct to the store and as the old man's living quarters. Books were everywhere here, jumbled in disorder, new editions and second-hand tattered copies in the same stacks.

Willy Forrest was past eighty; Runner had inherited him from his grandfather, almost as he inherited the big old mahogany desk in his apartment. The old man was perhaps the only close friend Runner had, although he saw Willy rarely. It had been two years, or close to it, since his last visit to the City.

"We will have tea," said Willy, taking the bag from Runner and stacking the groceries on top of the bathtub before finding places in the little kitchenette for them. The cover on the tub was the only flat surface, apart from the little stove, not piled with books.

He retrieved a box from the rutabagas and cabbage, set a battered old kettle on the stove. Runner was reminded of Agatha as he watched Willy putter about his kitchen. The old man produced a battered Coca Cola tray for the tea things when it came time to carry the service into the front room. Runner smiled at the tray; it had been in use for this as long as he could remember. Some modern collector would undoubtedly swoon over it now.

Pouring the tea, serving the lemon and cream, was almost a formal ceremony. He said nothing until Willy finished and sat back in his old, red plush Victorian sofa. The elderly man sighed as he sipped at the brew.

"Tea is life, James. In my younger days, I thought it was beer. Now I know better."

Runner held his cup in his lap, studying his old friend. Despite appearances, the bookshop was one of the most respected in America: Willy's twice-a-year catalogues went to a mailing list of several thousand occultists, as well as to all of the major libraries in the country.

"Well, James." Willy cocked his head to one side. "Why are you here? You've not come just to cheer up one old man, I know."

Runner considered the oath of secrecy he had taken years before when given top-secret clearance, his promise to Monaghan to keep the present investigation quiet—and told Willy Forrest everything. The man blinked when the story at last finished.

"This Olana Venedris, James. I have heard of her. An evil woman. A greedy woman."

"A customer?"

"I hope not. I would have to check the computer subscription list. I would prefer my money come from people not perverting the ancient wisdoms."

"She is only part of the conspiracy, Willy."

"That may be. What do you intend now?"

Runner shrugged. "I'm playing it as I go. First I want to check out Monaghan. Somebody told Olana I was coming to Boston, that I am investigating the deaths of the murdered agents."

"The Gemini Deaths." Willy Forrest sighed, closing his eyes. "Four sets of twins. James, I believe deeply in the powers of the hidden mind. To see them used this way . . ." He opened his eyes again. "The world is evil. As I grow older, I keep believing that each new generation will reject the ways of Satan. I keep thinking, I am an optimist. But it never happens. The struggle never ends.''

"Human nature doesn't change from generation to generation, Willy.''

"But the human spirit has the choice between good and evil. Why do so many choose the dark ways?''

It was an old argument, one Runner had heard in childhood. They sat together, talking of other things, catching up after two years apart. After nearly an hour Willy suddenly looked serious.

"James, I think you should call the girl with the amusing name.''

"Carla Twilty.''

"Yes. Call her now.''

"Intuition, Willy?''

"Perhaps inspiration. I think you should meet with Miss Twilty and her employer as soon as possible.''

The number was in Washington. The girl who answered said Miss Twilty could be reached at the Essex House in New York City. Runner called the hotel, wasted nearly five minutes fighting the switchboard before he was switched to the senator's suite.

"Oh, Dr. Runner!'' Carla Twilty's telephone voice had much of the same timbre as her mother's. "Mother called me this morning, told me you were coming.''

"I think we should meet, Miss Twilty,'' he said.

"My very thought. But there's no way I can make it this afternoon . . . tonight? Eleven o'clock?''

The women in his life lately seemed bred to late hours. Runner agreed to the time, hoping tonight's meeting would have a different outcome.

"Not here," she said. "There's a coffee shop down in the Village, Tomajoe's. On Bleecker Street."

"I can find it. How will I know you?"

"I'll know you, doctor. And I may have Senator Tucker with me. I hope."

He caught the concern in her voice as Carla Twilty rang off. Runner knew instinctively that he had made the right move, smiled as he replaced the receiver. Willy Forrest twinkled with amusement.

For a while they talked of old friends again; the time slipped by. Runner wondered why he stayed away from this old man so much when he so enjoyed Willy's company. Willy's days were numbered; there were precious few left. He decided to share as many of them as he could.

It was three o'clock. Time to call Vic Bremmer.

Bremmer picked up on the first ring. Runner identified himself.

"I'll call you back, James. Fifteen minutes. Give me the number there."

It was seventeen minutes before the phone rang. Runner grabbed it, growing impatient with the delay. He identified himself and heard Bremmer's sigh of relief.

"I'm in a phone booth, James. How long will you be there?"

"I don't know. It will serve as message center."

"Good." Bremmer sighed again. "Something is definitely up, James. I don't know what, though. I checked out your friend, was told at DIA he is out of the country. I tried to check on his Special Group and came up with nothing but a strong suspicion I've been given the runaround."

"Nothing more?"

"Nothing concrete. But I feel one hell of a storm getting ready to blow up, James. People at Langley are very nervous, and I know of no big flap now."

"Thanks, Vic. For what you have done."

"It's okay, old buddy. If I do come up with something more solid, I'll give you a buzz there."

Runner let the receiver drop, shrugged in explanation. "Nothing, Willy."

"I feel . . . nervous, James." The old man shook his head, blinking; he got up and moved a stack of books from the window, looking out into the street. "Something is wrong."

It may have been no more than suggestion, but Runner felt a crawling sensation across his spine. He stood.

"I think you're right. It's time to move on."

"You can't go in those clothes. I've some things you left here years ago, before you went to Vietnam for the first time. I'll get them."

Willy rummaged in a closet, came out with a package of shirts wrapped in blue paper, a pair of slacks in a dry cleaner's paper cover. The bottom of the paper was curling, brown with age. A shoe box gave up a folded sweater Runner had long forgotten and a neatly rolled pair of socks.

"I should have given you these before, James. Perhaps it was fate, my keeping them."

Runner changed clothes quickly; the old man bundled his discards together and tossed them in the same closet. Even as he dressed, Runner was suddenly bone weary. He was no longer a youngster. Strained muscles demanded the chance to rest, relax, recuperate.

But something definitely was wrong.

Bremmer.

The CIA man's words came back to Runner. Why was Bremmer interested in how long he'd be at this address, when he was only passing along information?

Runner transferred his wallet from his suit jacket, thought to check his money; he was low. He told the old man, who went into his bedroom and brought a strongbox back from a dresser drawer. He counted out five hundred dollars.

"Willy, you're a damn fool. Keeping that much money in the apartment."

The old man shrugged. "The neighborhood criminals think I'm a crazy old man, that no one ever comes in to my shop. I was robbed three years ago. They found two dollars in the cash register. Now they leave me alone."

The warning signals came louder. Runner shook hands with his friend and then stepped to the window, looking out again.

An unmarked car was double-parked in front of the shop. The men getting out might as well have worn signs saying cop! They approached the shop, one looking up toward the second floor window.

Runner ducked back. "Willy, is there a fire escape?"

The old man nodded. "Through the bathroom, James. Go up, across the buildings."

His last words were directed at Runner's back. It was time to start running again.

ELEVEN

Willy Forrest's building was considered advanced urban design when it was constructed in 1904. Willy himself was in knee pants in those days, coming up on his tenth birthday in the old country. His good parents would have been shocked to see the surroundings in which their son would come to the end of his days.

But that day was not yet, and Willy was aging better than his building. He didn't complain to the landlord, demanding repairs. Willy was his own landlord.

His bathroom was a closet no more than four-foot square. It held the toilet, which was at least as old as the building, operated by a chain dangling from a wooden tank overhead, and a porcelain sink on a pedestal.

The window in the back wall was a narrow rectangle of frosted glass; the latch had been painted shut twenty or thirty years ago. Runner saw instantly it was a waste of time trying to force it with his fingers.

He turned back. Willy was there, a hammer in his hand. The old man's eyes twinkled as he handed Runner the tool; he was having fun, perhaps for the first time in decades. He scurried away, to go downstairs and head off the official party that was already leaning on his doorbell.

The first hammer blow did no more than crack the thick paint around the latch. Runner tried again; the third blow moved it halfway from the catch. The fourth finished the job and Runner leaned his weight into the sash.

The window was stuck fast.

Gritting his teeth, he planted his feet more firmly and tried again, slamming the heels of both hands against the top of the sash. It broke free with a loud noise, rose an inch or so. He put his fingers under the sash, pulling up with all of his strength, and it rose another inch.

The frame had warped in its track.

Frustrated, Runner slammed his hands against the top of the sash repeatedly. After seven or eight blows the window finally broke free of the track, rose with a long protesting squawk.

Runner had grabbed his coat on the run. Now he turned back to take it from the sink, then pushed it through the window. He put his foot through, turning sideways. The opening was a tight squeeze; he wriggled through, took a deep breath and gagged. The landing was just over a row of garbage cans belonging to the sandwich shop. The stink was unbelievable. It hit Runner full in the face.

He stopped breathing long enough to shrug into the coat, and turned to lower the window. It stuck again. He growled, and put his heel on the sash. His weight was enough to force it down; anybody giving it a casual try would believe it hadn't been opened. He hoped.

Runner went up, breathing with his nostrils shut

tight. The fire escape was rusty and unsteadily pinned to the bricks of the building. It sagged alarmingly when he stepped onto the fourth floor landing and creaked loudly as he went up the rest of the way to the roof. But no one appeared in a window to complain.

He went over the top, landed on a six pack full of empty beer bottles; his ankle turned, painfully.

A dozen paces worked out the twist as·he threaded his way through the forest of TV antennae to the front of the building. There he leaned cautiously over the parapet, looked down. The two cops were just entering the shop; they didn't look up.

Looking about the roof, Runner took stock of his situation. There were several ventilators sprouting from the blacktopped tar paper, blades turning idly, and a square trap that led to the building's main staircase. Several of the neighboring buildings had low structures where the stairs came all the way to the roof.

That was the easy way down, if the doors were unlocked.

Runner crossed to the next roof, dropping almost three feet down from the parapet, and tried the stairs; the door was locked on the other side. He wasted no time moving along to the next building.

This had a trap door that wouldn't budge. To the next.

The door was ajar. As he opened it, Runner was hit in the face with seventy years of cooking odors, the stench of old urine. He slipped through, breathing through his mouth again, blinking at the sudden change from light to near darkness.

He moved cautiously down the stairs, met no one as he made his way down six flights to the lobby. The walls of the building were covered with scribbled graffiti, although there was almost no illumination to bring it out.

At the street, he looked out; the double-parked car was still there, with no sign of the cops. He opened the door and went out, turning south and walking briskly along. At the corner he turned west for one block, and then south again.

The hackles on his neck settled down. He was clear.

For the moment.

The problem was to stay clear, at least until his meeting with Carla Twilty. And the senator, if Tucker showed. But that was seven hours away. Until then he could do nothing constructive.

Bremmer had turned him over to Monaghan.

It didn't make sense.

None of it made sense, no matter how he tried to make the pieces fit. It was as though he was working with pieces from two different puzzles. The bright colors were the same, but the puzzles had been cut on different jigs to different patterns.

At times it almost seemed as though he could make them fit, if he just pushed harder. Forced them together. But the information that came out was meaningless. Gibberish.

Runner drifted east and south, knowing he had to keep on the move. Out of Yorkville, he was in unfamiliar territory. On 72nd Street he turned into a once grand picture palace, paid two dollars for admission to a double bill that promised excitement and allure. The posters were faded, the stars' names unfamiliar. It had been years since he had been to a Hollywood action program. Sandy Blake loved the movies, but pretentiously preferred foreign films, especially those with subtitles and murky plots.

He paused in a doorway to watch the flickering images for a minute, then went downstairs to a filthy lounge where he used the rest room. After washing, he examined himself in the mirror. His beard thickly stubbled his face; he felt tacky. Sticky.

He wanted a bath. He needed a bath.

A positive goal in mind, Runner left the theater without bothering to watch the film. He caught the subway to 42nd Street, took the shuttle to Times Square, came out and entered Liggett's drugstore to buy shaving equipment, toilet soap, toothpaste and toothbrush.

He crossed Broadway and Seventh Avenue, moved along 42nd Street, then paused to duck into a men's store and buy fresh underwear, socks, another shirt. After his bath the shirt so carefully saved by Willy Forrest would go into the trash. And the socks.

Runner moved toward Eighth Avenue and 43rd Street, turned into the Hotel Carter. It was called the Hotel Dixie in his college days; classmates wanting cheap quarters stayed there, along with the lesser lights of Broadway and the entertainment industry.

The Carter was tacky, as was everything else along the street, yet it still maintained a certain amount of dignity. The clerk behind the desk said nothing about the paper bag bearing the label of the men's shop, but informed Runner that a room with a tub was twenty-four dollars when he laid a twenty across the registration card. The false name and address weren't questioned at all.

The room was high up in the building, small enough

to give the nervous claustrophobia. It was clean enough, however, and the single window looked toward the Hudson River in the distance. The rooftops between were not the scene to be found on scenic postcards, but at least it wasn't an alley filled with garbage cans.

The water trickled into the tub, running brown for nearly three minutes before clearing. It was hot, though. Runner set the rubber stopper in place and went into the bedroom to undress. It was nearly ten minutes before there was water enough in the tub to satisfy him.

He stepped into the water, at first wincing at the bite and then sighing with pleasure as he lowered himself into the cloud of steam. One of the sybaritic pleasures in Runner's life came from soaking in a hot tub. He washed the dirt from his skin, then sank down, closing his eyes, to luxuriate in the heat. During his army days he'd often thought of retiring to Japan, a country that understood and appreciated the bath in all its nuances.

For a time Runner cleared his mind of the problems that had no answers. He thought of Willy; decided he loved the old man. The street punks thought Willy was crazy. What would they say if they knew that among the stacks of junk-wagon rejects, the knowledgable bibliophile searched for the odd illuminated four-teenth-century manuscript, or an eighth-century Persian fragment.

In Willy's bookshop were treasures that would be the envy of any museum in the world. And like any true bibliophile, Willy kept his finest treasures for himself, locked away where only he could see them and enjoy them. Twenty-five years ago Runner's grandfather said Willy's treasures were worth a million dollars or more.

Today, the cost of buying them on the open market would be incalculable.

*　　*　　*

Runner's eyes flew open; he'd been sleeping.

The water had cooled. He sat up, finishing washing, pulled the stopper with his big toe. After shaving, he stretched out on top of the bed, naked.

It was nearly five. Runner set the clock in his subconscious for nine o'clock and drifted into sleep again. He needed the rest. His body needed the chance to recover from the outrageous demands placed upon it today.

At exactly nine Runner woke again, refreshed and alert.

He sat up, checked his watch on the nightstand, then rose and dressed quickly. After waiting ten minutes for an annoyingly slow elevator, he was back on 42nd Street. He knew his destination, remembering Bleecker Street from visits to Greenwich Village in his younger days. He'd checked the address of the coffee shop in the phone book, called to verify the cross street.

It was still early; he headed for Times Square, intending to stop in Toffenetti's for dinner. But the restaurant was no longer on its corner. It had been replaced by a Nathan's Famous.

Not in the mood for fast food, Runner moved up Broadway to the first Howard Johnson's he saw and ended up leaving most of his food on the plate. Nathan's would have been better. He paid the check and left, still hungry.

It was time for the subway again. The token seller

sent him back to Eighth Avenue, where he took the A train to West Fourth Street, remembering the Duke Ellington song as he listened to the clack of the wheels.

He came out into a milling crowd on Sixth Avenue that reminded him of Boston's Little Italy on a festival day. People jostled and shoved him as he made his way along Eighth Street, moved down Bleecker to the coffee shop. He was still an hour early.

He spent the time wandering through the streets of the Village, over to Washington Square, along the buildings of New York University as it discharged thousands of evening students. There were strange languages in the air: Spanish and Chinese and the lilting singsongs of the Caribbean. The flavor of the Village was that of one of the old world cities, a constant bazaar where the tacky mixed with the exclusive, the tourist came to gawk and pay outrageous overcharges for handmade jewelry and souvenirs of New York that would be thrown into a drawer and never looked at again.

The night was cool; there were no chess players in Washington Square. Runner wandered to the entrance to Washington Mews, watched as an overdressed matron came out of her house with a Pekinese tucked her ample arm. She lowered the dog to do its business, then stopped to scoop up the remains, glaring at Runner when she straightened.

Poop went into a street trash container; dog went back under her arm. The matron turned and marched back up the steps to her house, head held high, haughty against the demands of an unreasonable world.

It was almost eleven. Runner returned to Bleecker Street, found Tomajoe's crammed with customers. Inside the door he peered over the heads of the customers, trying to spot Carla Twilty, or let her spot him.

He saw Senator Tucker first. They were in a booth at the very back of the place; Carla Twilty was a brown-haired imitation of Farrah and Cheryl and the other exponents of American enticement as calculated to raise the libido of the male population.

Runner threaded his way through the crush, apologizing again and again as he bumped chairs, nearly knocked a tray from a waiter's hand. Tucker spotted him first, rising to hold up his hand, as though offering a beacon.

"Doctor Runner!" Carla was on her feet, pulling her coat off the seat to give him room to join them. "I'm so glad to see you."

The coat was a fur jacket; the dress was something elegant in lime green. Both girl and clothes looked out of place in the coffee shop.

Tucker slumped into his seat, head hanging. There were lines in his face, bags under his eyes. His mouth hung open, and he stared into his drink as Runner sat down across from him. He looked twenty years older than his publicity pictures.

"Something to drink, doctor?" asked the girl.

Runner shook his head, turning to study her. Carla Twilty was nothing like the person he expected, after meeting Agatha. She seemed very young, hardly more than twenty, although her mother said she had worked for the senator for ten years.

His warning sensors were at work again.

He scanned the room, trying to pick out trouble, but none of the people around him carried the mark of policeman, of plant.

"Doctor Runner, we are in very big trouble."

Carla Twilty fumbled a cigarette from her purse, struggled with a lighter before she managed to get it lit. She drew raggedly on the smoke, let it trickle from her nose before saying anything more.

"Very big trouble," she said again. "You know its name."

"Olana Venedris," he said.

"Right, in a very big way." The cigarette stubbed against an ashtray, and almost immediately she brought the pack out and fumbled for another. "My mother thinks you can help us. Help Wendell."

Tucker raised his eyes at that, but still said nothing. Suddenly he raised his glass, gulped his drink. His throat continued to work when it was gone.

"What can I do, Miss Twilty?" asked Runner.

"Look, we can't talk here." The second cigarette broke as she slammed it against the ashtray. "Let's get out of this place, go some place safer."

The noise level was such that no one in the next booth could have heard their low conversation, but Runner shrugged and stood. He helped her into the fur jacket, forced a way through the crowd. Tucker trailed them like a forlorn puppy kicked by the master it loved. If he'd had a tail, it would have dragged the floor.

"A girl friend of mine has a place she lets me use," said Carla, once they were back on Bleecker Street. "God, look at this crowd! You'd think it was Saturday night. We'll have to go over to Sixth Avenue to get a cab."

She led the parade, Runner at her heels, Tucker dragging behind. Once Carla turned and spoke impatiently, almost scolding him. The senator, the man predicted by many political forecasters to be the next president of the United States, flinched away from her words, then hurried to catch up.

Carla Twilty was the sort of person only a mother could love. She would have to be good in her job, to make up for many people she would alienate.

Runner tried to probe her with his senses, but came up against a shell that seemed impervious. Hard, yet he knew it was brittle. It could be cracked, but what was hiding beneath the shell would not be pretty to see out in the open world.

His spine still crawled, even as they came out on Sixth Avenue. Carla stole a cab away from a tourist couple who carried the mark of Des Moines on their clothing and in their manner. Outraged, they could only stand speechless while she ushered the senator into the back seat, then waited for Runner to take the middle.

She gave the driver an address in the west twenties. The cab took off up Sixth Avenue, broken shocks jarring the passengers almost to the roof every time it crossed a bump. The driver jounced along with the others, never slowing as he swerved through gaps in the traffic, slammed the pedal to the floor to beat changing lights. The taxi turned west on 23rd Street, north on Ninth Avenue, went a block beyond the street of their destination and cut through to Tenth, then circled back to the address.

Runner released breath as Carla paid off the cabbie, and they both got out. The senator had endured the ride with hands folded between his legs, head bent over, as though he were on the way to his execution. He didn't move until Carla spoke sharply again.

"Wendell! Get out of the cab!"

The address was a green painted board door between two houses. Carla fumbled a key from her purse, looked up and explained, "Jen has the stable house. She's in Europe now, thank God. I need this hidey hole."

The street was lined with old brownstones. The building to the left of their goal had a brass plaque that said in scroll letters *The Conley Clinic*. There was no other information.

Runner didn't like the place. His sensors were screaming at full force. He took a step back, looked at Carla.

"Look, Miss Twilty—"

The automatic that came out of her purse was small, but nasty. The phallic symbol had no erotic interest for Runner as she pointed it with a steady hand, all nervousness gone from her manner.

"Inside, Doctor Runner. I know how to use this. Try something and I will."

Tucker let out a low moan that was almost animal in its anguish. Runner glanced toward him to see a dark stain spreading over the front of the senator's trousers. He whimpered, shaking his head.

"No, don't go in there! She isn't Carla!"

Disgust showed on the girl's face as she saw what Tucker had done to himself. She hacked, and for a moment Runner thought she was going to spit at the man.

He felt pity for the senator. And now he knew why the signals had been wrong from the moment he entered the coffee shop. This girl was not the one he had talked with this afternoon. And definitely not Agatha Twilty's daughter.

"Purely for curiousity," he said, mildly, "what is your name?"

She shrugged. "Christina. Inside."

Runner obeyed. He believed her when she said she knew how to use the gun. The age problem was solved; she was no more than twenty. But her years had been hard, showed now in her manner.

He moved along the alley, Senator Tucker stumbling behind him. It opened into a court that held a circular fountain; the water was shut off. Lights blazed from the back of the clinic, which shared the court with the four-story stable house.

Runner crossed the brick-paved court. A set of iron stairs led up to the second floor of the house; but the first floor was bright with lights. And now a door beneath the stairs opened.

Olana stood there, waiting.

TWELVE

"Ah! The prodigal returns."

The astrologer came out of the house, into the court-yard, smiling. Olana flicked her tongue against her teeth as she came closer to Runner, examining him from head to foot, stripping him naked with her eyes.

"Sooner than he expected," she added.

In that moment Olana Venedris looked like a predator in position to pounce upon an unsuspecting smaller animal. Her nostrils flared with excitement that was almost sexual, her eyes bright with anticipation. This hunter killed for enjoyment, not for food.

"You astonish me, James," she said. "Really. To come out of my spell as you did. You make me question my powers. I was quite embarrassed."

"You needn't be," said Runner. "You're a remarkable woman, Olana."

"And you a remarkable man. After last night, any ordinary male would have been exhausted. Paralyzed."

She moved around Runner, circling him completely.

Christina fell back, but the gun remained steady in her hands.

"I expected you to sleep for hours," Olana added. "Tell me, what did wake you?"

Runner shrugged. "You were noisy leaving."

"Oh, no." She laughed. "I was not. And you were out. Completely. I think a gun could have gone off by your ear without bothering you in the least. No, it was something else."

"Tell me what did it. I'd like to know, too."

"You're a senstive," said Olana. "A powerful one, perhaps the most powerful I've met. Your strength is astonishing, James. I guessed it before," she added, "but I wasn't sure. Not until I met you in . . . well, the flesh."

Runner heard a noise behind his back. He glanced around, hands out from his side in deference to Christina's gun, and saw two white-jacketed young men come out of the clinic. One was nearly as big as Ramsey; the other was closer to normal, but his short sleeves showed heavily corded arms.

Runner watched them approach, his eyes on the handcuffs dangling from the hand of the smaller musclemen. Then he looked back to Olana.

"For me?" he asked.

"All right, pal." The big man approached him, reached to force Runner's arm behind his back. "Be nice now, and we won't have to hurt you."

"Yes, James," said Olana. "Be nice. He hates you, you know. He'd like very much to have a reason for hurting you. Terribly."

"We hardly know each other," said Runner, mildly. But he was judging the strength of the two, wondering if he could throw the nearest against Christina. Use that as a diversion to take Olana.

"You killed his brother," said Olana. "And you've cost me Ramsey as well."

"I didn't kill Ramsey."

"So Agatha said. Still, he'd be alive if not for you."

"But I wouldn't be, if your original plans had worked."

"That was a mistake," she admitted. "Your . . . talents, for want of a better word, are much too valuable to waste, James. But I know some people who feel they can make full use of them."

Both of Runner's hands were caught now, the muscleman forced one up between his shoulders, until Runner winced, bit on his lip. One cuff snapped around that wrist, bit into the circle of flesh that was the scars caused by Mabry. They had barely healed.

Runner sucked in breath, winced again as his other hand was immobilized. The cuffs were too tight and the orderly kept pressure on his forearms. Very quickly the ache spread through his back.

Runner shifted his weight as the pressure made him rise on the balls of his feet. He could sense the tension flooding from the man holding him.

"He's hurting me."

"He may hurt you more," said Olana. "If I give him permission."

He stopped breathing, and the orderly relieved some of the pressure, enabling Runner to drop to a stance comfortable in comparison.

"Why did you kill Sandy Blake?"

The astrologer made an impatient gesture. "You

know the old saw, James. Omelettes come from broken legs. Believe me, I had nothing personal against the girl.''

''But you were after her brother.''

''Well, let's just say that her brother had become an annoyance some friends of mine could no longer tolerate. He was creating problems.''

''So you arranged his death.''

''I?'' Olana smiled again. ''I admit nothing. However, it would make an interesting experiment in psychic observation, wouldn't you say? Few siblings are really fond of each other, at least in the pampered society of this country. Twins are different. They are almost always close in relationships with each other. Someday I hope to extend the theory to triplets, even quadruplets.''

''Why was I involved?''

''Happenstance, James. Or fate. Whichever you prefer.''

Olana's attention switched to Senator Tucker. She took stock of what the man had done to himself and her expression turned to intense disgust. A mewling sound rose from her throat and Runner thought she was going to strike him with her hand.

''Good God, look at you!''

''Olana, please . . .'' Tucker whimpered as he spoke her name and one hand came up in supplication. He had been crying, silently.

''You disgust me!'' snapped the astrologer. ''You turn my stomach! You, you dare say you wanted to be president of your country! If your voters could see you now!''

She turned away, snapped at the other orderly. "Take him into the clinic, clean him up! Remember, he has to make that fund-raiser tomorrow evening."

"Yes, ma'm."

The orderly took Tucker by the elbow, urging him along. He stumbled. "C'mon, Senator Tucker, let's go have ourselves a nice bath. And then you can pop into bed and sleep it all off."

"Olana! You promised!"

The lament was a wail as Tucker took a single shuffling step along. The astrologer's face showed disdain.

"Give him a shot," she ordered. "Anything to stop his whining."

Senator Tucker followed the orderly, slipping his hand into the younger man's like a little boy holding to his mother. They reached the steps; Tucker stumbled on the first. The orderly had to help him up the stairs and across the back porch of the clinic. As he weaved along the senator moaned.

Runner watched until they disappeared, then released pent-up breath. He wheeled on Olana, wincing as the man holding him yanked him back, made him stumble.

"What have you done to him?"

"Very little," she said, disinterest in her voice. "The man is a complete fool. He was born a fool."

"You have him hooked on something."

"He addicted himself. Percodan. He took it for years, as much as fifteen or twenty tablets a day when he came to me. An old spinal injury. It's really surprising he managed to put up so strong a face to the public without something embarrassing happening before now."

"Percodan doesn't do that to a man," said Runner.

Olana shrugged. "He needed something stronger. I have access to . . . certain people. Some of them are working with experimental drugs. Very good drugs, in some cases. They almost work miracles."

"What is Tucker taking?"

"I don't think it has a name," she said. "Not yet. It worked, you know. Cleared up his pain problems overnight. Unfortunately, it has a few side effects."

"Including a total change of personality?"

"Oh, Wendell never had a personality. Not a real one. He's a mimic, responding to what people want to hear. The best politicians are mimics, you know. Have no souls of their own."

"What is going to happen to him?"

"For a while, nothing. He needs increasing dosages, of course. At the moment an injection every six hours is enough. He doesn't really deteriorate for another twelve hours after missing the shot. Most of the time he's the man the public always thought him to be. He can go on like this for years. At least a few years."

"By which time he'll have run for the presidency."

"By then he'll be the president," countered Olana. "He will win, James. We have the money and the organization to make sure of that."

"He'll be a puppet," said Runner. "Under control."

"Completely. Even now Wendell can't choose a pair of socks by himself. But there will be someone at his side at all times to help him make his decisions. And he'll still put out a good image."

"You'll lose control, if he dies in office."

Olana shook her head. "No. The man who succeeds

him will be one of our own. This time we can't lose."

This time. Had there been other times?

Runner blinked, wondering who her companions might be. He hadn't missed, when she spoke of Americans as though they were another people.

He ached; he wanted relief. He arched his back against the pull of his arms, felt pain through the cords crossing his back. But Olana wasn't ready to release him. The astrologer seemed in an expansive mood. Runner decided to probe further.

"Who is *we*, Olana?"

"Ah." She smiled again. "Let us just say I belong to a group of concerned citizens. Concerned with the future of America, and the future of the free world. We, our group, would like to believe the promises of the politicians, but they lie. Why shouldn't they lie, when their only goal in life is to keep in power? So we do what we can, working with them when possible, against them when not. We have managed to . . . adjust the trends, shall we say?"

A young black man came out of the house; he was slightly built, not at all like Ramsey. He coughed discreetly, three paces away, until Olana turned.

"Washington, Madame." He glanced at Runner, let his eyes flick back to the astrologer. "On the telephone. The call you were expecting?"

The look of irritation disappeared; Olana nodded once. "It's about time. All right, Gordon, you can take him upstairs. You know what to do."

"One question!" gasped Runner as the orderly yanked back on his shackled wrists.

Olana turned back, eyebrows lifted. "What is it?" she demanded, impatiently.

"What happened to the real Carla Twilty? The one I spoke to this afternoon?"

"Are you sure you didn't speak with Christina?" she asked, showing amusement.

"I'm sure. I should have tumbled sooner tonight."

"Christina is an excellent actress. Like your politicians, a perfect mimic. Carla is safe, James. Wendell is fond of the girl, though I'm sure I don't understand why. She is safe. As is her stupid mother."

Then Agatha had been found out as well.

Runner felt suddenly deflated. As he studied the astrologer, he knew their safety was a thing of the moment, subject to change at whim.

Olana was capable of anything. In spite of his pain, he opened his senses to the astrologer, knew she had taken delight in planning the macabre deaths. The Gemini Deaths, as Willy Forrest had called them.

He also knew Olana was a power in her organization. She carried authority and used it. She was not the one to accept the commands of others.

She did turn, then, and disappeared toward the house. Before Runner could see her go in, the man holding him twisted his arms, forced him to swing in a circle that turned into a trot toward the stairs. He lost his balance, stumbled, cracked his knee against the rough surface of the first metal riser. Runner gritted his teeth against renewed pain as the man yanked him erect. Air wanted to explode from his lungs. He made it trickle out as the orderly butted him in the ass, made him move up the stairs.

Marching at quick step, they passed through a stainless steel kitchen where two nurses in crisply starched white dresses shared coffee before going on shift. One was colored café au lait; the other was Spanish American. Both raised an eyebrow, but said nothing as Runner was pushed through a set of swinging doors.

There was no respite; the orderly yanked him around, marched him up to the third floor, into a room. At the last minute he gave his prisoner a shove that sent Runner sprawling across a hospital bed.

The handcuffs were released; his arms fell forward, sharp pain coming from the jaw bites. Runner had no strength to move as the orderly tried to make him stand.

"Goddamnit, undress! You bastard!"

He was helpless, his hands did nothing more than flop loosely as the orderly cracked him across the face. Runner tasted blood, felt new pain when his nose broke. The rush of blood came stronger.

The orderly continued to curse as he forced Runner around and around, undressing him roughly. Soon he was naked; the man pushed him onto the bed, which bore a single sheet with a rubber square spread across the middle, and stretched him out.

Leather straps went around his wrists, around his ankles. The orderly pulled on the straps until the cords in Runner's joints hurt anew. Then something cold went over his hips, stretched across his lower belly, was cinched tight to the bed.

"Now try something!" The orderly looked at the prisoner, shaking loose hair from his sweating eyes. "Get out of that, if you can!"

Suddenly he slammed his fist into Runner's stomach with all of his strength. Runner felt the explosion of agony through his entire lower body; he was sure he had heard the crack of his pelvis. He tried to rise up against his bonds, but he was tied too tightly.

"I ought to kill you, you bastard!" said the orderly. "But that would be too easy. I don't know what they're planning for you, but I hope they slice your nuts off with a rusty blade and make you eat them!"

The man stared at Runner for another minute, breathing raggedly; the prisoner was afraid to close his eyes, afraid of what the orderly might do. Then he was gone, and Runner could sag within himself, deflated.

His face fell away. The blood was still running, although slowly; there was a large sore spot inside his cheek where he had bitten himself. One tooth seemed to be cracked from the blow to his face.

He slept.

*   *   *

Cool water brushed his fevered brow. Runner opened his eyes, saw the black nurse; she had a basin, a cloth, was cleaning him up.

"God, I needed an angel just now."

The girl smiled, but said nothing.

Runner tried again. "Do you have a name?"

No response. She moved down his body, did some things Runner couldn't see, but felt. There was a sting of astringent, the heavier feel of a coating of ointment, the lighter touch of gauze. Some of the touches came where he hadn't realized he was injured.

"I think I'll call you Mercy."

The girl spun around, eyes wide in astonishment. She glanced toward the door, then approached to lean over him, forming soundless words with her lips. *How did you know my name?*

The room was bugged; Runner nodded to show he understood and managed to form a smile.

"You're an angel of mercy. That should be your name, no matter what you were christened."

The nurse smiled as she left the room with her tray. Runner rolled his head from side to side, examining what he could see of his surroundings. The walls were painted the usual hospital green, the color supposed to tranquilize the emotions; bright cheery curtains hung over what must be a window, although they were closed.

The orderly had moved the bed table out of the way while strapping Runner down; it was just in the corner of his vision, toward the foot of the room. A small metal cabinet served as bedstand, a rest for a telephone, although the instrument wasn't there; he saw the jack receptacle just above the top of the cabinet.

A florescent fixture in the center of the ceiling was bright in his eyes; the four bulbs were protected by a plastic grid. The lights in the panel over the head of the bed were also bright. Runner blinked, tried to shut them out; they hurt his eyes.

It was easier with his eyes closed, although there was a constant redness behind his lids. He sucked in breath that hurt his lungs. His kidneys also hurt; he had to relieve his bladder. After the sucker punch, he was afraid there'd be blood in his urine.

Time passed, dragging. Runner tried to shut out the hurting, tried to concentrate on Olana and what she had said. The organization was more powerful than suspected—if their plans were advanced far enough to elect their puppet to the Oval Office.

What were Tucker's chances, assuming they did manage to keep him propped up? For the first time he regretted ignoring politics as he had. Runner had resigned his army commission because he could no longer stomach the double dealings of politicians, not when he carried guilt over the death of the patrol with a sense of moral outrage. At first he had believed when the brass hats and the politicians said America was justified in going into other countries.

He had been politically naive; it hurt to think how stupid he had been. Wave the flag and James Runner reacted. Tell him the Pope was a card-carrying Communist and he'd be ready to storm the Vatican.

Now the Pope came from a Communist country. And now he knew that everything they had fed him for so many years was pablum, intended for the feebleminded great American public. He no longer believed in anything except in being left alone.

But he was involved in this, like it or not.

Olana had brought him into it when she decided to eliminate a brother named Sam Blake by killing his sister.

Maybe Olana's power group would be no worse in the long run than the ones now in control. Runner didn't know, didn't care. Olana's people had struck at him, treated him as no more than a nuisance, set him up to hang for murder simply because he was there.

He was involved.

He hadn't chosen a side; Olana did it for him.

Monaghan might be another of her puppets; if so, Monaghan would have to watch out for himself. For twenty years James Runner was trained to be a fighting machine, taught the many ways of killing another human. For the past seven years he had tried to live another life, live in peace. But others said no. They saw him there, a pawn on a playing ground, and moved him about for their own purposes, not caring what he thought.

Runner reacted. Olana had thought him a cipher, a meaningless neutered thing, a mule. She gave him a burden.

Now he would give it back.

Somehow.

*　　*　　*

Runner screamed.

He rose in bed, arching against the straps that held him, eyes wide and staring as pain stabbed through his genitals. His nostrils flared wide in panic and he tried to twist away from the claws digging between his legs.

"Oh God!"

Olana released him, laughing. He sank back down to the bed, sucking in flat breaths as the astrologer moved up to where he could see her face. She sat beside him. She was naked. "Really, James! So tender, so helpless." She patted his cheek. At last he manged to ask, "What time is it?"

"Does it make a difference? But I will tell you: just after two." She reached beneath his sight, captured him again; this time she only stroked him. "I must admit, James, I wasn't going to come to you tonight. But my curiosity has been piqued. I wanted to test your strength again."

Suddenly she rolled away, bent over him. Runner sucked in breath as Olana took him into her mouth. Despite his hurting, he was quickly aroused.

"Ah, that's better." She sat up again, then crossed

over his hips, facing him; she sat back. "Now let's try it like this." She sighed. "Oh, yessssss . . ."

Olana pleasured herself with Runner's body, ignoring his gaspings and moans of pain. He twisted against the straps holding his wrists, tried to turn his hips away: all without success. Her weight was incredible; she was destroying him. Killing him.

Finally Olana rolled free, dropped to the floor, caught up a robe from a chair. She knotted the belt, tossed her hair from her face, laughing. "You should have enjoyed it, James. It may well be the last woman you will enjoy, you know."

She slipped her feet into mules very like those worn by Sandy Blake. "In the morning you'll be taking a little trip, James. Out of the country. To a nice safe place, where my friends can really study this remarkable ability of yours."

She moved away, turned back from the door when Runner called her name.

"Yes, James?"

"Monaghan. What did you give him to turn mole?"

"You mean that ridiculous man with the red hair?" She laughed. "He isn't one of ours, James. Wherever did you get that idea?"

"Your memo pad. You had his room number at The Ritz-Carlton."

"Well, we keep track of fools as well as enemies, James. A fool might get in the way by accident, but the damage he causes can be annoying."

With that she was gone, leaving Runner in a state of confusion.

Monaghan wasn't a mole. Unless Olana lied now, he

could have saved himself a great deal of trouble by going to the Irishman in Boston.

But someone was feeding information about this operation to Olana's people. If not Monaghan, who?

*   *   *

Runner's eyes opened again; he'd been asleep no more than twenty minutes. His internal clock was working again; it was half an hour since Olana had left him for the night.

Someone was coming.

The person paused in the corridor, listening. Runner opened his senses, probing: a woman. A friend.

The black nurse came in, stopped when she saw he was awake. Mercy held her finger to her lips and Runner nodded; she came closer, bent to place her lips against his ear.

"Mister, I don't know who you are, but I'm blowing seven months' work infiltrating this operation. I sure as hell hope you're worth it."

Mercy straightened, fumbled with the straps holding his wrists. She moved down to release his feet and then undid the strap around his hips.

"Where are my clothes?" he whispered, sitting up and rubbing his wrists.

He swung his legs out of bed, winced, reached to Mercy for support. She hung onto him until he could stand straight.

"I don't know," she said, also whispering. "They weren't planning on you wearing them out of here. I've got a set of orderly's whites stowed at the nurse's station."

He staggered to the door, gaining strength with each step. Adrenalin flooded into his bloodstream, his mind drawing in this time of danger on the reserves in his body.

"Can you make it?"

"Yes. How did you get the message to help me?"

"My dear old Mama." She smiled. "These people are nuts on security, but stupid, too. When I came to work I told them Mama was a nutty old woman who was gonna bug me three or four times every night. I'm good at my job, gave excellent references, so Doctor Conley decided to put up with it. For awhile they listened, but now they don't bother."

They were halfway to the nurse's station, which was around a corner. Mercy's voice rose a tone, although still soft.

"I told Mama you were here when she called the first time. Ten minutes ago she called back and told me to get you out of here. Man, I gotta say it again, I sure as hell hope you're worth blowing the set-up."

"Who are you, Mercy?"

"Immigration and Naturalization. The clinic is a front for smuggling some very big name mafia-types in and out of the country. Conley's a plastic surgeon," she continued. "A lot of them leave with new faces. Hey! Take it easy!"

Runner's fingers had dug into her arms.

"Someone's coming," he said, tensed. "From downstairs."

"Oh, shit! That blows it."

It was too late to retreat. Runner moved forward, dropped to the floor; he peered around the corner. The muscleman was coming up.

Runner pulled back, closed his eyes while he sucked breath, summoning strength—and exploded around the corner just as the orderly came off the stairs.

His rush caught the man by surprise; he threw a block into his gut, threw him back down the steps. The man somersaulted back, rolling over and over, making an ungodly racket as he crashed all the way to the foot of the flight.

"Oh, sweet Jesus!" said Mercy, coming up. "Now what?"

"Is there another way down?" demanded Runner.

"The elevator. It's on the ground floor."

Reinforcements were downstairs. The orderly let out a groan, and somebody shouted. The man was stunned, but not out. Runner heard other voices, the pounding of feet.

He couldn't go down. There were too many of them.

The only way out was up.

He moved quickly, leaving the nurse to care for herself. There was one more regular flight of stairs: at the top arrows pointed to X-ray and Surgery. Beside the arrows an iron ladder led up to the roof.

Runner took the rungs at a leap, scuttling until he reached the trapdoor. There he paused to slam the heel of his hand against the latch.

It popped free on the second blow. He raised the trapdoor, stuck his head out and was hit by raw November wind that blew across the rooftops. Runner's teeth began to chatter and he started to retreat.

A gun exploded, below. The bullet burned a crease across the cheek of his ass.

Expelling breath, he rose through the trapdoor, swung out onto the roof. He slammed the trapdoor shut, looked for something heavy to weight it down. There was nothing.

He was trapped on the roof.

Naked.

THIRTEEN

Runner was in near darkness, although to the north, the east and the south the city was ablaze with lights. This was Chelsea; there was nothing west of here but other blocks of brownstones and the river. A string of lights marked the Westside Highway, while down near the tip of the island the World Trade Center's twin towers rose into lowering clouds.

The wind cut through him, chilling Runner until he lost feeling in his extremities. He crouched low for protection, as lights flooded the courtyard behind the clinic. There were voices.

Concentrate!

Runner ignored the cold as he closed his eyes, pushed hurts and pains from the aware level of his mind to some deeper place where they couldn't intrude. Now he opened his senses, probing the night, listening with his mind . . .

Escape. Go west.

He came up onto three points, opening his eyes again, his vision was better adjusted to the night. He broke into a low run that avoided unseen obstacles in his path, zigzagging without conscious thought.

A shot rang out, sang into the night as he went over the parapet between the buildings. He moved quickly before the gunman had a chance to take bearings and come fully out of the trapdoor. Runner swerved through the forest of TV antennae, cut around a pool of broken glass that glittered, would have cut his feet into hamburger. He leaped a second parapet and then a third, ran for the fourth—

He stopped with his hands on the wall, looked across thirty feet of vacant lot to the next building. The lot below was strewn with rubble from the demolished building that used to stand there.

Another shot rang out, missing him by thirty feet. There were more people on the roof of the clinic, although none as yet showed an inclination to follow him across the rooftops. They milled about, talking in low voices that carried clearly: they waited for someone to tell them what to do.

That someone would appear shortly: Olana, if no one else had the authority.

Runner stood near the front edge of the building. A chimney blocked him from view of the posse. He rose far enough to peer over, then ducked back. The street below was deserted, but there was no way to get down.

The side overlooking the vacant lot was no better.

There had to be a fire escape.

He dropped low again, skulking, crawled almost on his belly toward the back of the building. A powerful beam of light shot out suddenly, bobbing erratically. Someone had produced a spotlight, but as yet they didn't know how far he had come.

He found the fire escape before the searchers reached the first parapet, went over the edge of the roof in a sinuous motion, reaching as far down the supports of the ladder as he could while the curved tile on the parapet was like ice across his groin. The light bobbed nearer; he swung down on his hands, gasping when his feet hit the bars of the iron landing.

He moved to the stairs. Stopped. A window opened off the fire escape, a bedroom. A night-light gave a feeble glow through an open door. Someone was in the bed. Two someones.

Runner tested the window, found it locked. Moving down the stairs, he glanced at the window on the fourth floor landing as well. It was closed and blind, a window shade pulled tight against the bottom.

Down again. His teeth were once again chattering, almost uncontrollably. He could hardly feel the railing of the fire escape under his fingers. A shiver started that grew to shake his whole frame.

He stopped once more, unable to proceed; he doubled over, wrapping his arms tight about his chest. The window jiggled back and forth before his eyes with the shaking of his head. Gaps showed at the top and the bottom, two inches in either position.

Runner lunged for the bottom gap, got his fingers beneath the sash; it rose smoothly in its track. Before it stopped he dove through the opening, landed on thick shag carpeting. The voices were closer now, almost to the edge of the last roof.

Summoning a final reserve of energy, he came to his feet, pushed the bottom of the window shut. He started to do the same with the top when a querulous voice broke out behind him.

"Hey, what the—"

A girl sat up in the bed, hugging the blankets to her breasts. Sleep-befuddled, she stared at the naked man by the window. As Runner spun, he saw her mouth gape open, saw the scream start to rise from her throat.

He dove for the girl, bounced across the bed to slam his hand across her mouth. The fire escape rattled beneath the first of his pursuers.

The girl twisted against him, shocked at the touch of his icy body. Runner thrashed with her a moment, managed to get on top.

"Please! I'm not going to hurt you!"

"Mmmm! Mm!"

"I'm not a rapist," he said, hurriedly. "Those men are after me. They want to kill me! Please, you have to help me. I'm begging you."

She nodded, and he took his hand away from her mouth; started to clamp it back again when she sucked in a deep breath. But she wasn't trying to scream.

"Get under the covers!"

Runner rolled over, dug deep into the bedding as the girl pulled it over his head. She settled herself again as the first of the pursuers landed heavily on the fire escape. They spoke softly, but their words came clear through the gap in the window.

"He's gone!"

"Impossible!" said another. "He has to be around here somewhere."

"You tell me where, then. I tell you, he made it to the street."

"Without clothes? He must be damn near frozen already."

"Then somebody'll find his corpse in the morning. I tell you, he made it away."

"She won't like it," said the first voice, darkly. "She's going to have a lot to say about this."

"Let her find him, then. I'm going back. I'm cold."

"No. Keep going. We'll have to search the area. She won't settle for a half answer."

The men moved past, three, four, there was a loud creak as someone stepped on the bottom ladder and it sank slowly to the alley below. Then the noise repeated again as it came back into place, followed by a loud complaint.

"Assholes! Get outa here before I call the cops!"

A window slammed; the voices moved away in the alley.

Silence returned.

Runner shivered beneath the blankets, unable to control the trembling. The girl on the other side of the bed moved closer, put out a hand to touch him.

"Jesus! Are you okay?"

"H-h-hot! Hot water b-bottle! A-anything h-hot!"

She understood. The girl rolled out of bed, naked, and dug into the bottom of her closet and came out with a box. While Runner tried to curl himself into the smallest possible ball, she pulled an electric blanket from the box and shook it out over him.

She straightened the folds in the blanket, found a wall receptacle for the plug, turned the dial on the control to maximum.

"My mother sent me this for Christmas three years ago," she said. "Damn thing is too heavy, I hate it. I'm gonna fix you some soup, okay?"

Runner didn't answer, conserving strength. He was

numb in every extremity, felt the cold as a physical presence in his gut. The shivering wouldn't stop. His body had lost too much precious heat. Moving had saved his life.

The blankets covered his face; only his eyes were exposed. He saw a light come on in the next room, heard the girl moving about. Suddenly she realized she had nothing on and gasped.

She came back to the bedroom. "Don't look, dammit! Why the hell didn't you say something?"

She found a robe, went back into the other room. Heat began to spread through the circuits of the blanket, soaked through into Runner's outer nerve endings. Sensation began to return, the surface layer of his skin tingled, began to itch, began to hurt.

The girl came back with a heavy mug; steam rose from it as she settled on the edge of the bed.

"Instant soup," she said. "Split pea. It was the quickest thing I could think of. Can you sit up?"

Runner still shivered, but he tried a tentative shift of his feet—stretched out. The girl doubled the pillows and moved them under his head, then turned away to snap on the light of the nightstand. When she turned back again, she sucked in breath.

"Jesus! Somebody's really been beating on you."

Runner managed to worm a hand from beneath the blankets, got it around the mug. He lowered his face to sip at the hot soup, sighing as the steam filtered through his nostrils.

"Are those guys law?" she demanded.

Runner shook his head. "No."

"Yeah?" She examined him suspiciously. "What about you? Are you a cop?"

Two ounces of soup were down. Runner sank back into the pillows, sighing again; his eyes closed. The girl punched his shoulder.

"Dammit, are you? If you're a cop, I want to know."

The trembling eased; his teeth stopped chattering. Not opening his eyes, Runner felt the aura of the girl beside as a warmth separate from the heat returning to his body. He sensed her suspicion, knew she lived by a strong moral code of her own that decried what she considered to be the oppression of the establishment.

"No." He opened his eyes. "I'm not a cop, Miss—"

"Cindy. Cindy Kaflin. What's your name?"

"James. James Runner."

"Well, Jim, whoever the hell you are, it looks like you got yourself some big trouble. Who were those guys chasing you?"

"Bad people. Very bad people."

"Hey, I get it! You were cutting in on their territory, so they tried to ice you, huh?" She shrugged. "What was it, coke? Hey, I hope it wasn't hard stuff, man. I mean, each to his own and all that, but hard stuff is dirty."

"It wasn't hard stuff."

Cindy swung her legs around, worked them beneath the blanket again. "They play rough, huh? I mean, I know this is New York and all, but chasing a bare-assed guy across the rooftops is not exactly an everyday occurrence. At least, not in my life."

Her foot brushed his leg, moved away. Moved back again. Cindy reached to turn out the light, then slid the rest of the way under the covers. She popped back out long enough to take off the robe and throw it in the general direction of the closet.

When Cindy slid beneath the blankets again, she moved close enough to take Runner in her arms.

"I'm sorry, Cindy," said Runner, sleepily. "For dropping in on you like this."

"Hey, that's okay."

Cindy giggled; her hand stroked his chest. Runner was still cold, but he could draw heat from the girl now as she settled down until her face was against him. The hand moved down farther, exploring.

"I'm sorry," he said again a moment later. "That's nice, Cindy, but I'm afraid it isn't going to do any good."

"Hey, that's cool, man. Everything's cool."

*   *   *

Runner's eyes flew open. The room was dark, but daylight filtered around the edge of the room-darkening window shade that had been pulled to the bottom of the window. For a moment he was disoriented, then everything came back.

The girl was gone; he was alone in bed.

The smell of coffee hit him in the gut; he sucked in a deep breath, suddenly ravenous, and sat up. The extra bedding had been removed, sat folded in a chair. The electric blanket was turned to low.

"Cindy?"

She appeared in the door; she wore jeans and a paint-smeared sweatshirt.

"Hey, Jim. Ready for some breakfast?"

His automatic clock was working again; Runner knew it was midmorning. "I'd love some."

"How'd you like your egg? I'd like to say eggs, but I only got one left. Plenty of bacon, though. And toast."

"Scramble it," he said. "Please."

He threw the blanket aside and got out of bed, stretching. His body still felt the effects of the night, but he could operate.

In the light, after he raised the shade halfway, the room was grubby, everything unwashed. The smell of old sweat came from Cindy's closet and the sheets on her bed looked as though they hadn't been changed in weeks, if not months. His skin crawled; then he remembered that she had taken him in and he shrugged off the feeling.

He found the bathroom. "There's a fresh towel and a new cake of soap," called Cindy from the other room. "I figured you'd want a shower. If you can take the pain, there's a new Daisy razor on the sink. The shaving cream's low, though."

Runner spent twenty minutes under the shower. Cindy waited until she heard the water stop before breaking the egg in the frying pan. When he came out he smelled the food and was hungry all over again.

He wrapped the towel around his hips, went in to sit at the grubby table while she served up the food, poured coffee. Runner ate quickly, appreciatively, not bothering to make conversation until he sat back, finished.

"I really want to thank you, Cindy. For everything."

"Hey." She shrugged. "You're a good person, Jim.

I can tell. Good people have to do things for each other. It's the only way, right?''

In the daylight he examined her. Cindy was almost pretty. With a little effort she could have made herself attractive. Her breasts were small, but her hips were full. He remembered the touch of her body in the bed and glanced down in embarrassment at the towel.

Cindy laughed. ''It's cool, Jim. I won't hassle you. Either sex happens or it doesn't. Last night was the time, and you were in no shape. Now if you're here another night, that's another story. You got a place to go now?''

''Yes. But I need clothes.''

''There's some stuff my boyfriend left a while back. It probably won't fit too good, but it's better than nothing.''

She followed him into the bedroom, rooted in the closet and came out with a torn gym bag. It produced a pair of paint-spattered flannel trousers, a sweat shirt, a pair of torn sneakers. The pants were three inches too big and two inches too short, but the belt cinched them in. Cindy dug farther, came out with a field jacket almost black with grime. It was too tight across the shoulders, but he managed to button it.

''I'll get this stuff back to you, Cindy.''

''Hey, throw it in the garbage.'' She laughed. ''You don't look like Beau Brummel, Jim.''

He glanced around, spotted the phone he'd seen earlier. ''Now I have to make a few calls.''

''Sorry, it's dead. Ma Bell cut me off six months ago. She wants three hundred bucks deposit to turn it back on again. That, and the hundred I owe on the old bill.''

Cindy dug into her jeans, came out with two subway tokens and two dimes. "This I can let you have, Jim. Sorry I can't do better."

"You've done more than enough, Cindy. Thank you. I'll be back to repay you."

She seemed embarrassed. "Hell. Take it light."

Runner caught the girl as she turned away, pulled her into his arms long enough to plant a single kiss on her lips. Cindy blushed deeply, then melted into his arms with a low sigh, began to rub against him. Her arms went around his neck and she took over the kiss.

"Wow." He broke out of her arms. "Cindy, I will see you again. I promise."

"Yeah, sure." The girl turned away again, didn't watch as Runner opened the door. "See you."

Runner suddenly felt his age as he went down the stairs, wondering if he would keep his promise. Cindy was perhaps nineteen.

He turned up the collar as he went out of the house, conscious of the cold against his stockingless feet. He glanced toward the clinic; a man in a trench coat lounged against the house across the street from it. He glanced toward Runner, then away as Runner turned toward Tenth Avenue.

He found a phone booth on the next corner. Miraculously, it wasn't out of order. He dialed Willy Forest's number, listened to it ring a dozen times.

The warning sensors were working again as he let the phone drop back into the receiver, fished the dime out of the slot. Willy should have been in the shop. Home. That he wasn't, was disturbing.

Something had happened.

Runner looked out of the phone booth at the stream

of uptown-bound traffic, gnawing on his knuckle; his mind was far away. Everything he had touched lately had gone sour. Every time he went off by himself, he ended up deeper in hot water.

He wanted Olana; wanted to hurt her.

He slumped, covered his eyes with his hand and let his senses probe the house behind the clinic, the clinic itself. There were people there, but all were strangers. None of the auras were hostile.

The astrologer was gone.

He opened his mind fully, sought the touch that was his old friend in Yorkville. Nothing. And when he let his thoughts soar wide, there was no touch that was remotely like the gypsy woman's.

Monaghan.

There was no one else left.

Olana said Monaghan was not part of her group. Had she lied? He didn't think so. There was no point in lying about the Irish agent.

Runner dropped the dime again, dialed the operator and charged a call to Boston to his home number. The Rtiz-Carlton operator answered on the second ring.

"Is Philip Monaghan still registered in 817?"

"Just a moment, sir. I'll check." The woman came back. "Yes, sir, he is. Do you wish me to connect you?"

"Thank you, yes."

This time there was no answer for nearly a minute. After the eighth ring Runner was ready to hang up; the phone spoke in his ear on the ninth.

"Yes?"

The voice was a stranger. "I want Phil Monaghan."

"Doctor Runner?" The voice in Boston sighed in

relief. "Jesus, where the hell are you? The roof's about to fall in and Phil's screaming for your hide."

"Where is he?" said Runner.

"In New York. Wherever you are, sit tight. We'll send a car to pick you up."

"I'm in New York. What's his number? I'll call him."

The voice in Boston gave him the number and Runner dialed it, using his dime again. A pleasant voice answered.

"Federal Bureau of Investigation, good morning."

He asked for Monaghan, was put through almost immediately. Someone else answered; Runner identified himself and the agent came on, screaming.

"James, where in the sweet name of Jesus are you, you dumb son of a bitch?" Monaghan was so upset he forgot to use the insulting nickname. He screamed again when Runner told him his location. "You dumb bastard, you mean to tell me you're still near the Conley Clinic? Get your ass over there! And stay there!"

Runner let the phone drop, shook his head as though water was in his ear as he walked away. When he returned to the street just left, three men were out on the sidewalk, waiting for him.

They let him say nothing, took him into Conley's private office. For the next twenty minutes he cooled his heels, until Monaghan came exploding through the door. The Irish agent used his hands like an Italian as he called Runner ten kinds of an idiot.

"Are you finished?" asked Runner, quietly.

"Yes." Monaghan dropped into a chair, wiping spittle from his mouth. "All right, I've calmed down.

182

Now will you please tell me just what the fuck goes on in that head of yours?''

Runner told him everything that had happened. By the time he finished several other men had crowded into the room, listening intently. They looked in awe as he described last night's escape over the rooftops.

''And that's it,'' he finished. ''Except for one thing: Who is the double agent?''

Monaghan looked away, embarrassed. ''Somebody high up, Jamie.'' The bantering nickname was back. ''Somebody so high up, it hurts. Clement Castagnola.''

Runner blinked. ''The president's personal assistant?''

''He's been serving as the president's deputy to the National Security Council. He got all the reports as soon as they came in. I guess I spilled most of it myself.''

''How did you tumble?''

''One of his girlfriends figured he was trying to dump her. She knew he had been taking classified material to her apartment, left some Top Secret stuff there overnight. She called Jack Anderson and he called Castagnola at eight o'clock this morning. It's on the news bulletins right now, 'Clement Castagnola blows out brains.' ''

The Man in Washington. A very important man. The conspiracy had already infiltrated the highest levels of government.

''What about Wendell Tucker?''

Monaghan shook his head to Runner's new question. ''He wasn't here when we blew this place this morning.

If you'd stayed put another hour, Jamie, we'd have cracked you out of there, along with Madame Olana. The whole lot of them cleared out, except for the hired help. Conley, too.''

Mercy Plymouth, the nurse, had managed to stay out of the way until the order came from Olana to abandon ship. Runner felt relief at that. He'd been afraid she was going to have to pay for helping him.

"They've dropped out of sight," said Monaghan. "The lot of them. We're watching the airports and terminals, alerted the border patrol if they try for Canada, but I'm afraid she made it clear, Jamie."

Runner shook his head. Eyes closed, he had remembered the Westchester estate mentioned by Agatha. He couldn't probe that far, but he was sure Olana had gone there.

He opened his eyes again, blinking; he studied Monaghan. He wasn't going to tell him about Westchester.

Willy was there. And Agatha and Carla Twilty. Runner knew that as certainly as he was sure he had located the astrologer.

Let Monaghan go in, in force, and Olana would kill them all.

FOURTEEN

Runner knew he was going after Olana.

Alone.

But it would be suicide to try a daylight attack on the Westchester stronghold. His mind turned over a score of plans while the agent pumped him for another half hour for more details of what he had done. Then he yawned in Monaghan's face.

"I'm going to bed. I don't want to be disturbed for the next twenty-four hours, unless the hotel is on fire."

"All right, Jamie." Monaghan sighed. "But we're back to square one. You're sure you've no idea where she might have gone?"

"Out of the country, for all I know," he said.

"It's possible. INS ran a check on her, they think Olana is actually a woman named Zora Buczek who was deported about seven years ago. If so, she's about four years older than she claims to be. They don't know when she came back into the country."

Runner's clothes had been found at the clinic, along with his wallet. Willy's money was gone, but his credit cards had been left untouched. He changed as quickly as he could, then arranged with Monaghan for some cash to tide him over.

He called three hotels before finally securing a reservation at the Waldorf-Astoria. Monaghan sent word to Boston to ship his bag down from The Ritz-Carlton on the next shuttle, and provided a car to take him uptown.

At the hotel, he checked in, then looked up the address of the nearest business office of the telephone company. Runner caught a cab to the office, identified himself to a company representative as a customer in good standing and with solid credit. There was no question when he said he wanted Cindy Kaflin's overdue bill charged to his home number, or when he guaranteed payment of future bills.

Ma Bell was satisfied. She didn't care who paid, just so long as she received her due. An order was put through to reconnect Cindy's telephone at the local office, the promise made that it would happen immediately.

Runner left the phone company with a lighter conscience, but his errands had just begun. Next he went to Brooks Brothers, supplemented his wardrobe with dark clothing and a fleece-lined short jacket, leather driving gloves. From there he visited a hardware shop.

The purchases returned to the hotel, Runner grabbed a cab to the nearest supermarket, filled grocery bags with all the intriguing gourmet items he could find. Another cab took him to a florist's on Lexington Avenue, and then to a candy shop on Fifth.

Thirty minutes later the taxi pulled into the street of the clinic; the trenchcoated watchdog had disappeared.

Runner stopped the cab in front of Cindy's, where an aging Puerto Rican woman smiled widely and held the door for him after he struggled up the stoop.

On Cindy's floor, Runner raised his knee against her door, balancing one bag of groceries while he knocked. The door opened so quickly he nearly lost everything, stumbling forward. Cindy just saved the flowers and the candy.

"Hey, Jim!" Her eyes grew wide. "I had a feeling you were coming back. But what's all this?"

"Christmas," he said.

"Hey . . ." Cindy shook her head, blinking. "You didn't have to do this—five pounds of candy! Jeez, I haven't had five pounds of chocolates since I broke into my sister's piggy bank when I was eleven."

She turned away to safely put the candy on the table, the flowers across the kitchenette's sink. When she turned back again her hands went across the sides of his throat, and she kissed him, gently.

"You didn't have to do this."

"You didn't have to take a bare-assed nut into your bed in the middle of the night," he countered. "You did, and you saved my life." He smiled. "Why don't you answer your telephone?"

"Huh?" The phone rang. Startled, Cindy spun around . . . dove for the instrument, digging it out from under a pile of discarded magazines and clothing. She fumbled the receiver to her ear and listened then laughed.

She shrugged when she hung up and came back to Runner. "No, I don't want ten free disco lessions."

Cindy kissed him again; she had bathed, shampooed

her hair, changed to clean jeans and a soft sweater. She smelled of lemon and strawberry. Runner noticed she had changed the sheets on the bed.

"I figured you were coming back, Jim."

After they were beneath the covers Cindy moved against him; her hand roamed his chest, exploring.

This time her explorations brought results.

* * *

Midnight. Runner switched off the lights of the Cutlass after he U-turned, came back a quarter mile and let the car coast to a stop at the side of the narrow country road. The villages of Bedford and Bedford Center were a mile away, Pound Ridge only a few miles farther.

The road was paralleled by a high stone wall. Warning signs posted every two hundred feet said: Danger! Electrified Fence. High Voltage.

Runner had retrieved the car from the Yorkville garage after leaving Cindy, and after three hours alone in his bed in the Waldorf. He wore the dark clothing, the jacket; his hardware purchases were coiled on the floor in front of the seat, steel grapple hooks affixed to the end of fifty feet of light hemp rope.

He wore rubber-soled shoes. A sheath containing Hoffritz's finest skinning knife was on his left hip. This time Runner had come prepared to scale walls.

He was armed as well. Monaghan provided a pistol without comment when asked. The .38 Police Positive snubnosed revolver in his jacket pocket seemed a heavy weight. Runner hoped he wouldn't have to use the gun, but the weight was partly balanced by the extra box of shells in the other pocket.

The wall was nearly half a mile long; there was one gate, five hundred yards ahead as the Cutlass now was headed. A sign on the gate gave warning that the grounds were patrolled by guard dogs.

Time to move.

He slipped on the new driving gloves, gathered up the rope and slung the coil over his shoulder. There was a moment of alarm as he opened the door and the dome light came on. He should have remembered to remove the bulb.

Clouds obscured the sky, but were breaking in several places. Runner started to cross the road, then ducked back: there was the roar of an engine, coming from Bedford, and then headlights rose above a rise in the road.

It was the first car he had seen since scouting the road. He ducked behind the Cutlass, dropped to the cold damp ground; leaf mold pressed around his hands, chilling them through the gloves.

The roar of the engine came again as the driver shifted up and down, erratically. Then a battered old pickup truck appeared, weaving from lane to lane. As it passed the car, Runner saw a woman, slumped against the wheel and steering with her forearms. The truck nearly went into the ditch, and then she recovered. The truck disappeared.

He went back to the car, dug behind the seat, brought out a rubber bathmat, the largest he had been able to find in the hardware store. He rolled it, stuck it into his jacket, pulled the zipper up to keep it in place.

Crossing the road, Runner slipped the rope into his hand, loosening the first coils. He swung, casting carefully: the hook bounced off the edge, fell back with a jingling noise that seemed loud in the still night.

Runner tried again; the grapple caught on a stone. He set his weight against it, planted his feet against the wall—and the hook dug through rotten grout and popped out.

Runner swallowed a curse as he sat down, nearly rolling backward over his head. He recovered quickly and moved along the wall, surveying it more closely. The grapple would have caught easily on the back of the wall, but he was afraid the wire might break an alarm when the rope weighed it down against the top.

A larger stone than most protruded farther than its neighbors. Runner licked his lips as he gathered the coil for another try—threw the grapple. It looked as though it was going to twist free. He pulled down and the hook caught, firmly set behind the stone. He flicked the rope an inch to the right and the grapple turned over, another hook catching as well.

Runner went up quickly, wrapping the rope around his hand when he reached the top. With his butt still hanging down between his heels, he pulled the bathmat from his jacket, shook it out, slipped it beneath the wire and over a sea of broken glass that glistened in the moonlight.

Bouncing two or three times with his hands only inches from the grapple, Runner swung up and straddled the wire. His foot came down on the mat at a precarious angle; he nearly lost the rope as he fought for balance, got both feet onto the mat and onto almost level footing.

Runner released his breath, changed his mind, and bent to retrieve the rope. When it was in his hands he peered into the shadows at the base of the wall; the moon had slipped behind a cloud cover again.

The ground below was in total blackness. The tree was about twelve feet away, a gnarled oak—its branches rose into the night, bare of leaves and ghostly. One reached almost to the wall, but nearly five feet over Runner's head. Another angled away, nearly ten feet higher but almost straight out from the trunk.

A low growl sounded in the shadows of the tree.

Runner froze, hackles rose on his neck as the Doberman gave its warning. Almost immediately there was a single questioning bark in the distance. Half a minute later the other dog came loping along the wall to join its companion.

The grapple swung loose in Runner's hand, as he stared at the dogs; it dangled about eighteen inches. The pendulum movement attracted their attention as they came to an attack position a few feet from the wall. The Dobermans were dark masses in the night, relieved only by bright eyes glowing and by yellowed teeth gaping in their mouths. Then the moon broke free, illuminating the man straddling the wall and sheening the coats of the two dogs. One growled again.

Runner raised his eyes to look toward the house. It was a dark bulk on top of a knoll, a good five hundred yards away. At first he saw only a single lighted window on the second floor. Then he picked out a fall of light through tall windows at one end of the first floor.

Behind that was the darker shape of a high-peaked garage. In the moonlight, the house revealed itself as built in the Tudor fashion: half-timbered and dormered.

The blacktopped driveway circled an enormous stone planter in front of the house.

Runner looked again at the branch just above his reach. The limb tapered down, was no more than an inch thick at its closest. If he could reach it, it was much too brittle to support his weight.

He switched his attention to the other branch and eyed it carefully. Gathering the coils of rope again he swung the grapple around his head four or five times and let the rope lengthen with each pass.

The grapple sailed out, fell over the branch; momentum wrapped it several times, securely. The limb swayed when Runner tested the rope, but was strong enough to support far more than his weight.

He filled his lungs with air, launched himself away from the wall. Excited, the Dobermans spun on their heels as they saw he was going to pass to their left. One leaped, jaws slavering, and Runner's feet slammed the animal's shoulder. The Doberman was thrown straight back, hurled into the trunk. It bounced away, yelping, then subsided to whimpering as it fell with broken bones.

The second dog tried to halt in midleap. Its head snapped around, missed Runner's heels by inches. It landed, wheeled to leap again, but the man was in the tree, hanging precariously over the branch near its juncture with the trunk.

Runner scuttled up the branch to the place where the rope had coiled. The limb was only four or five inches thick at that point. It swayed beneath his weight, bent toward the ground as he freed the grapple and pulled the rope away from the infuriated dog. The dog leaped again and again, falling inches short each time.

At last the animal stopped trying. It took up guard stance, eyes red with anger as it glared at the man above its head. Runner coiled the rope, let the grapple dangle.

"Ah, ah!" he said, softly, as the Doberman leaped again. "Not yet . . . not . . . yet!"

He let the grapple swing lower and wider; the Doberman's head moved with it. The dog rose from its haunches, tensed for another leap, and Runner yanked the hook out of reach of its teeth.

"Once more," he said. "Come on . . . once . . . more"

The grapple swung out almost five feet father. This time the Doberman was successful, but the dog didn't see the man let go of the rope. The rope snaked out, following the weighted hook, while Runner shifted his hands to grab the branch from one side.

He swung down from the branch as the dog sailed past. His feet bounced off the animal, knocking the Doberman askew. It fell on its back, kicking wildly, as the man landed on his knees only a few feet away.

The Doberman rolled completely over, came to its feet and launched itself for Runner's throat just in time to receive the skinning knife square in the chest. Runner grunted with the force of the blow. The dog's eighty pounds knocked him straight back, stabbing pain through his arm. The animal sank its teeth into the man's forearm . . . as the knife came out of the hole in its chest. But the attack was only reflex; the Doberman was already dead.

Runner raised his numbed arm, the knife was loose in his fingers. He picked it free with his other hand, sank down on his knees and ran the blade into the ground.

The other Doberman growled.

He fell back on his haunches at the renewed menace, saw the broken animal trying to scrabble toward him. Runner came to his feet with a shake of his head. He took a single step, staggering, then circled the animal, coming at it from behind while the dog tried to snap around at him. The knife severed the arteries and cords in the throat, cutting off the final growl with a gurgle of spilled blood.

The man sat back again, wiping his brow. He cleaned the knife of blood, running it a dozen times into the damp ground. The chill quickly seeped through his knees and his legs. He sucked in half a dozen deep breaths, chest hurting, and forced himself to stand.

Runner listened. There was nothing to indicate an alarm had been raised. The house was too far for anyone there to hear the small sounds made by the dogs.

He sheathed the knife and felt a stab of pain in his knee. The fabric was ripped, the skin beneath scraped. He wondered idly when it happened: when he hit the branch, or when he fell to the ground.

No matter. He was in and the dogs were dead.

Now for the house.

FIFTEEN

As Runner approached, other lights were visible on the first floor, most of them leaking from behind wooden shutters. Runner dropped to the ground at the bole of the last tree, a maple. His knuckles touched a protruding root as he opened his senses, probed the house.

Within seconds he touched the blazing aura that was Olana. The astrologer was agitated, angry; she was pacing, a half dozen steps back and forth, in the room with the tall windows.

Runner swallowed, tasting bitterness; his throat seemed dry. He let the touch of the gypsy woman slip away, although its heat was still there, as he passed through the rest of the house . . .

Willy was on the second floor. The old man was weak, but he seemed at peace. Perhaps he was asleep.

Runner penetrated further, touched strangers. At least a dozen of them were scattered through several rooms on the ground floor.

In the midst of the strangers, he suddenly touched the

rot that was Wendell Tucker. The mind brush almost sickened him.

Now he scouted the rest of the house with his fully extended senses. Reaching again to the second floor, he came on Agatha, a fluttery spirit that jumped about beneath his touch. A stranger was in the room with her, a woman. Although new, the touch was almost familiar: Carla.

The daughter's aura was tormented. She was resting, but beneath the surface attempt to relax was an anger as strong as Olana's. Agatha was dozing, lightly.

Runner left the women, tried to encompass the entire house in his mind. He was seeking a way in. As earlier in his career, he had unknowingly used his sixth sense to find a way out of danger.

The first floor was guarded; he sensed that the doors were locked. He left the maple, circling the house. As he came all the way around, he noticed a glitter over the peak of the garage's roof. An attic window.

The glass of the window reflected the moonlight as the clouds broke completely and scattered. To the south was the glow of New York City, but to the north the sky was black velvet, spangled with stars.

Only the top two thirds of the window broke moonbeams to shards; the bottom six inches were black. The window was open. Reachable, from the roof of the garage.

A low shed sprouted from the rear wall of the garage, a roof supported on stripped four-inch saplings. The shed held four-foot logs for the house's fireplaces.

Runner came closer, found a pile at the end of the row to use to vault onto the shed's roof. From there it was only a step to the steeper pitch of the garage, which rose to only six feet below the open window. A single leap hooked Runner's hands over the sill; he didn't need the rope.

He pulled himself through the window, raising it farther with his shoulder; he dropped the coil of rope just inside the window when he was through.

Dust exploded into the air when his feet touched the floor, scuffing across a narrow aisle of spilled moonlight. Particles entered his nose. He smothered a sneeze, but almost immediately another blasted loudly.

Runner froze. He listened with ears and probed with his mind to see if the noise had alarmed anyone below.

There was nothing. Except for the prisoners, everyone was on the first floor. Wendell Tucker was on the first floor, in a drugged stupor.

Runner moved forward, almost stumbling. He closed his eyes, paused to let his sixth sense take control, guide his way through the jumble of junk strewn across the attic, which was a single open room running the length of the house. Despite the open window, he soon was sweating enough to open the jacket.

He found his way to the stairs, moved carefully down a dozen steps. At the bottom, the door was closed.

Runner paused again, listening; then eased it open. The stairs opened onto a hall that crossed the long axis of the second floor. It was brightly lit by half a dozen wall scounces.

He moved out; only a few feet to his right the stairs came up from the first floor, twin staircases rising on either side of a twenty-foot wide entrance hall. A wide landing circled the well, and from the first floor rose voices: two men, complaining together.

Runner listened to the griping a moment, then turned

back into the corridor. Doors opened off either side; beyond the first was Willy Forrest.

He opened the door, slipped into the darkened bedroom. Runner stood with his hand pressing the line where the door met its jamb, listening. Across the room, a night-light burned near a large canopied bed. The room was frilly, meant for a young girl.

At first there was no indication of life in the almost insignificant lump in the bed. But the aura was there, weak and elusive. Runner moved close to the bed, saw a gentle smile wreathing his old friend's face, heard the faint hiss of his breath.

Willy's head was bandaged; he had been injured.

Swallowing anger, Runner moved away, listened at the door with hearing and with mind before moving out. The two women, mother and daughter, were across the corridor.

They slept lightly. Runner opened the door, slipped into the room, hit the wall switch.

Carla sat up, befuddled, blinking against the light.

"Who the hell are you?"

Runner held his finger to his mouth, warning her to be silent as he sensed an explosion coming. Then Agatha sat up in the other twin bed, staring around the room. She was even more confused than her daughter.

"Doctor Runner!"

Agatha's hand jumped to her mouth as she gasped out his name; Carla relaxed, let out a sigh instead of the scream she had planned.

"The hero," she said, with amusement. "Thank God! We were about to give up hope."

Runner recognized the strong tone of sarcasm. He studied Carla Twilty a moment before replying. She was in her mid-thirties, but strongly handsome. He could see Agatha in her features, knew that she would resemble her mother even more in another thirty years.

Both women wore frilly nightgowns that didn't fit. Agatha's was too tight. Carla's was loose, but her figure showed well in the folds of the garment.

"What happened to Willy Forrest?" he asked.

"Who's Willy Forrest?" asked Carla.

"Do you mean the little old man they brought in last night?" said her mother. "I heard Dr. Conley say he had a serious concussion. This morning," she added, glancing at a clock radio. "Oh, dear! I mean yesterday morning. Everything's happening so fast!"

"Not fast enough for me," said Carla, swinging out of the bed. Her breasts arched high as she stood.

But Runner missed them for the moment. His eyes had closed, in pain. That was why Willy seemed so much at peace. He knew the old man was very close to death.

His eyes opened again. "Are the guards armed?"

"Some of them," said Carla. "A guard patrols the upstairs every thirty minutes, looks in each of the rooms. He's due soon."

"He has a machine gun," said Agatha, nervously.

Runner let his mind probe again. He caught one of the men he'd overhead earlier. The man's thoughts had moved to the prisoners. He'd be coming this way soon.

"All right." He stepped back, hit the switch; the room plunged into darkness unrelieved by the bare amount of moonlight that fell through the two dormers that overlooked the front of the house.

"Please go back to bed, Miss Twilty. Pretend you're sleeping, both of you."

Carla shrugged, climbed back into bed. But they held themselves taut, their breathing seemed preternaturally loud. If the guard listened, he'd know they were faking.

Runner moved to the wall by the door, shifting a chair out of the way. Now that the moment of action was at hand, he had become quiet, waited patiently. Excitement before, release after, combat. Always remain calm during the actual attack.

A minute passed. He sensed someone coming up the stairs, heard footsteps. The guard entered Willy Forrest's room.

Agatha's eyes stared toward the door, wide open. The guard moved on, coming closer. Runner started to say something, but it was too late. The knob turned and the door swung in.

The old woman closed her eyes, shutting them tight, screwing up her face. The guard remained within the gap, hand on the doorknob, but not close enough for Runner to take him without risking alarm.

Carla moaned, turned over; through slitted eyes she saw what was happening. She moaned again and pretended to wake.

"Oh!" She glanced toward the guard. "Oh. It's you."

"Everything okay, ladies?"

Carla yawned, stretched. "It's stuffy in here. Would you be a doll and open the window? I can't sleep." She added a small laugh. "I'm not planning to jump out, you know. I know about the dogs."

The guard laughed with her. "Sure, I'll open it. Brutus would just love to sink his teeth into your sweet meat, though. I saw him and Devil rip a town punk to pieces, 'bout two years ago. Stupid kids.''

He came into the room still talking. Runner moved behind him as the guard crossed to the window, leaving the door open for the light from the hall. Runner had sensed that suspicion was lacking in his thoughts.

"Gah!"

The faint protest was cut off almost immediately as Runner's forearm yanked him back, slammed him across a raised knee. The fall was muffled by the thick rug, but the man arched his back against the clutching hands, started to drum his feet as his windpipe crushed beneath Runner's thumbs.

"Oh, dear!" said Agatha, sitting up again. "Is he . . . is he all right?"

"He's dead," said Carla, satisfied, as she came out of the bed again, approached Runner. "You are good." She bent, scooped up the fallen M-16 rifle. "Now let's see what we can do together."

"We're doing nothing," said Runner, rising and grabbing the semiautomatic weapon from her hands. "Use this and you'll bring down the whole damn army!"

Carla resisted his pull, breath hissing through her clenched teeth. Then she surrendered the rifle, Runner almost falling back in reaction.

"You're right. I'm not a fool, Dr. Runner. Tell me what you want us to do."

"That's better," he said relieved. He checked the gun, returned it to safety. "Describe the first floor to me. The room where Olana is most likely to be."

"If she's still downstairs," said Carla, "the library.

Her bedroom is at the far end of the corridor.''

"She's downstairs," said Runner. "Most of them are. Only you two seem to be in your bedroom."

"Wendell?" asked Carla. "Where is he?"

Runner detected the strong note of anxiety, sensed that Carla Twilty deeply loved the man for whom she worked. Too bad she wasn't a sensitive, couldn't probe the rot in his soul . . .

He shook off the thought. If Carla stayed with the senator, she would soon learn what sort of a man Wendell Tucker had become.

Then he wondered if the rot were of Olana's doing. Perhaps Tucker had been spoiled all along. If so, then he did feel sorry for the woman who had devoted a major portion of her adult life to the wrong man.

"The layout downstairs . . ." he said.

Carla Twilty gave him the information requested, calmly, going over several points again when he raised questions. The emotional outburst of a moment ago seemed under control, although Runner knew that she still seethed. In three minutes he knew the house as though he had lived there.

"You're good," he said, approvingly.

"I've been coming here with Wendell for the past two years," said Carla. "This is the first time I've been a prisoner." She paused, then added, "I only hope you're half as good as my mother thinks you are."

"So do I," said Runner.

He didn't wait to see if Carla was going to obey his orders. No matter her feelings, she was no fool.

He moved down the hall again, paused for a moment outside of Willy's door. There was no reason to enter. The life force was hanging on, very weak. It could wink out at any instant, but there was nothing Runner could do for his friend until matters had been settled.

He reached the stairwell, listened. No one was about in the foyer. No one had come to check on the missing guard.

It would happen soon. Runner crossed the landing quickly, moved to the back of the house where stairs led down to the pantry. The kitchen was dark, he passed through swinging doors into the dining room when he heard someone coming from the front of the house.

There was only one man. Runner heard the refrigerator door open, slam shut. He rose far enough to peer through the porthole in the service door, saw the man seated at a counter with a sandwich. His back was turned.

Runner slipped into the room, this time the door creaked as it swung shut. The man at the table started to turn at the noise—caught the chop of Runner's hand across his throat, took the skinning knife in his belly.

The man went back, arms loose. A bottle of orange juice tipped over when his head fell against it, slid across the table to crash to the floor before Runner could catch it.

Cursing silently, he lowered the dead guard to the floor. The man was unarmed. He straightened, moved to the other set of swinging doors just as two men came from the front of the house, arguing.

"I tell you, I heard something."

"All right, we're checking it, ain't we? Jesus!"

The second man carried an M-16. Runner ducked back, glad the dead man hadn't turned on the lights. No point heading through the dining room. They'd see the body as soon as they came into the kitchen.

He moved to the side, waiting, wishing he had thought to bring the M-16 from upstairs. At the same instant he spotted a fire axe on the other side of the door; there was just enough time to retrieve it.

The men came through together, without caution. Runner held the axe in both hands, slammed the butt against the face of the man nearest him. The guard went backward, his M-16 clattering to the floor, his nose and mouth smashed. Blood poured into his eyes as he hit the floor, screaming.

The other guard sucked in breath, but lost it again as Runner's shoulder took him in the gut, slammed him back against a worktable. Pots and pans rattled, then crashed to the floor from the bottom shelf as the guard's weight tilted the table onto two legs. Before he could recover, Runner kicked him in the face.

The two were out of action, but the alarm had sounded. Others were coming now, feet running. Runner spun around, grabbed the M-16 and pushed into the dining room as reinforcements rushed into the kitchen. He heard angry shouts as he moved on into the hall again, came back into the kitchen behind the four men who were bending over their fallen companions. Runner opened fire.

One man had an automatic in his hand; he managed to get off one shot before he died, the military slugs tearing through his face and making mincemeat of his brains. The others never had a chance to raise their weapons as the semiautomatic rifle tore them apart.

The M-16 was empty. Runner was nearly deafened from the sound of explosions in the stainless-steel quarters of the kitchen. Bullets had ricocheted in every direction, tearing through refrigerators and freezers, clanging pots hanging from racks over the table and the twin ranges. There was a stink of burning insulation.

Runner gasped, almost shivering, as he realized the rifle was empty. He spun around, reaching for the .38; it was gone. Fallen from his pocket, perhaps when he came out of the tree.

Pilot lights flickered on the nearest stove; chrome had been scarred by bullets, but there was no smell of escaping gas. Runner moved to the gory mess that was the pile of bodies, fumbled until he found a .45. It might have been the one fired at him; the barrel was hot. The clip was full, except for the expended bullet.

A rifle muzzle poked through the gap between the swinging doors. Runner saw it, dropped flat as the gun fired, shot once. He heard a gasp of pain. The doors sagged and the gunman fell dead, his face torn apart by the bullet from Runner's Colt.

Eight down. Nine, counting the man he had taken upstairs. How many were left?

Agitated, Runner tried to probe the front of the house, but his sixth sense failed him. He couldn't even locate Olana. His own thoughts were roaring, cutting off any outside impressions, no matter how strong.

Runner bent low, approached the crack in the door from one side. He had a clear view over the body to the front of the house, but no one else appeared. He was sure there were at least two or three more, plus the astrologer. Where the hell were they?

The hall past the dining room was inviting: a clear highway to death. Runner resisted the temptation. He moved back, found the door. Someone had turned on the floodlights. The lawns were flooded all the way to the nearest trees.

No way to get through that sea of light. Runner forced himself to breathe slowly, trying to calm his thoughts. The stink of released body waste rose from the corpses behind him. It was a smell he had not encountered for more than seven years, but one he would never forget.

The hall, too, was a certain trap. There was only one thing left to do.

Runner retraced his steps through the pantry, up the back stairs, around through the second-story corridor. He dropped flat near the stairwell . . . sucked in breath as Carla stuck her head out of her room.

"Get back, damn it!" he called, in a low voice. "Stay covered!"

Her eyes widened as she saw him; then Carla nodded, scuttled back. Runner breathed a sigh of relief. Idiot woman!

He wormed on his belly to the railing surrounding the stairwell. Downstairs, the front door stood open. He heard the stutter of a car engine as someone tried to start it, failed.

Olana? Immediately Runner knew the astrologer was still in the house. In the library. She wasn't alone; his recovering sense probed the first floor, felt two men with her.

One was Wendell Tucker.

A car door slammed; another chunked open. The person outside had given up on his first choice, was going to try another.

Runner went down the stairs quickly, crossed the foyer, glued himself to the wall outside the library. The door was closed, but he could hear angry voices. One was Olana's. The other he didn't recognize.

Tucker was conscious, but only barely.

A door opened from this corridor, into a conservatory. The floodlights from outside picked out white-iron summer furniture in a profusion of plants. Beyond, he could see more light coming from an open door of the garage; then another door opened and the man moved back to the car he had managed to start.

They'd be coming through in just a minute.

He bent low, ran down the hall, into the conservatory. It was glass-walled; french windows opened onto a patio, as did others from the library.

Runner waited until the car came out of the garage, tires squealing, then ran through the windows. He could see Olana in the library; she had Tucker's arm, was urging him toward the door while the guard with her checked cautiously for Runner. The door was cracked no more than an inch as he tried to scout the hall.

Runner reached for the outside knob; the windows were locked. He drew back, raised his foot, kicked the fragile doors inward.

The guard turned, shocked. The .45 tore through his throat. His hand tightened on the rifle, sent a line of bullets through the fine old paneling of the ceiling as he slammed against the wall, then slumped over.

"Damn you!" cried Olana.

Runner spun, saw the gun she held against Tucker's throat. He froze in the act of shooting.

"Get back, or I'll kill him!"

Runner expelled breath, suddenly deflated. Tucker was rotten, but he was a senator. An elected representative of the American people. He couldn't risk his death.

"You can't win, Olana."

207

"Oh, we'll win," she said, sneering. "It's fate, James. The stars predict our success. Every oracle I consult is in our favor."

"You've already lost."

"No. This is only a temporary setback. A single mistake. We'll recover. There's bound to be small mistakes in a plant as big as ours. We will recover." She was sure of herself.

Now the other guard returned from starting the car. He was astonished to see Runner; he raised his weapon to fire, but Olana told him to put it down.

"We need you, James. You're the strongest sensitive I've ever seen. We have to know what makes you tick. Throw your gun over here."

Runner shrugged, obeyed; he turned at her command, heard the guard rummage in a desk drawer at Olana's order. He saw the handcuffs in the man's hand as he came up behind Runner; this guard didn't try to punish him with the jaws. Once they were firmly caught, he was satisfied."

"We're leaving, James," said Olana. "Sooner than I expected. Stagg, take care of the three upstairs. The women first."

The guard left; a moment later a single shot rang out upstairs, followed ten seconds later by a second. Then there was half a minute of silence, followed by a third shot.

"Olana?" Tucker raised his head; he had soiled himself again and his eyes were like two sunken coals. "What have you done?"

"Shut up, Wendell. I've no time for your nonsense."

"*What have you done?*" he said, quavering. "*Tell me!*"

The strength of his outburst startled her. She looked at Tucker in surprise; then she laughed.

"Only what needed doing, Wendell. Now be quiet. We're going to take a nice ride, then get on an airplane. I'm taking you to a place where doctors can put you back together again. You still want to be president, don't you?"

The library door slammed open, startling all of them.

Carla stood there, an M-16 in her hands.

"Wendell!" she ordered. "Get down on the floor!"

Tucker obeyed, dropping away from Olana's gun as the astrologer spun to meet the unexpected challenge. The gypsy hesitated a fraction of a second, unsure of which one to shoot first—

And was thrown back, cut completely in half by the spray of bullets from the M-16. Carla held the trigger down until the gun was empty, riddling the ruined remnants of Olana's once beautiful body long after she was dead.

"Carla . . ."

Runner sucked in breath, ready to shout the command that should have stopped the woman from her act of vengeance. But the word stayed in his throat as he saw Wendell Tucker roll away from the line of fire, crawl with surprising strength on his belly to escape.

"We needed her," said Runner, softly. "We needed the names she could give us."

Carla raised her eyes to his. "But she deserved to die."

"Yes," he admitted. "Probably a hundred times over. That's why I didn't try to stop you. I just hope the price doesn't prove more than we can afford to pay."

SIXTEEN

A month later Runner sat alone in the cramped office he shared with a very young assistant professor; many of Runner's graduate students were older than his roommate. The university had closed the day before Christmas. Virtually everyone else had left; Runner faced reluctantly a pile of student term papers that needed grading.

Footsteps sounded in the marble corridor. He closed his eyes, probed the visitor.

"The door's open, Monaghan," he called, when the knock came. The agent opened the door came in.

"Jesus, Jamie! Is *this* what you call an office?"

The agent shook his head as his eyes skimmed the disorder of the room, the battered twin desks shoved together, the two wooden file cabinets that had been there since the university was still a college.

"What do you want?" said Runner, wearily.

Monaghan pulled books from a straight chair, swung it around, sat down with his arms crossed over the back. For a moment he eyed the other.

"You did well, Jamie," he said at last. "It's too bad Carla Twilty got carried away, but overall, Washington is satisfied with the outcome."

Olana's part of the conspiracy was broken. Willy Forrest had finally regained consciousness and was recuperating in a private hospital near New York City. Runner was flying down to spend the holidays with him. Talks with Willy's doctor had produced a tentative promise that he might be able to take him back to his apartment in a few weeks.

"I'm glad Washington is glad," said Runner, sarcastically.

"Did you hear about Senator Tucker?" asked Monaghan, unperturbed. "His resignation?"

"I heard."

Agatha Twilty called him with the news. Tucker had announced his withdrawal from public life, disclaimed any future interest in elected office. Ill health was given as the reason. It was close enough to the truth.

Immediately after the press conference, Tucker left the country for an extended vacation at an undisclosed location. He was accompanied only by his personal assistant, Carla Twilty.

"She'll marry him," said Agatha, on the telephone. "I think it's what they both need, Doctor Runner. I think they'll be happy together."

Runner said something noncommittal before hanging up. He could sense only trouble for that marriage. The rot had eaten too deeply into Tucker's soul for him to ever find happiness, and the knowledge that he had come to the pinnacle of political power would fester like an untreated sore.

"I've been promoted, you know," said Monaghan.

Runner raised an eyebrow. "The group's been given permenent status, by Executive Order. I'm the head honcho."

"What do you want from me, Monaghan?" asked Runner, for the second time.

"The job isn't finished, Jamie. Olana was only a part, and maybe not a very big part, at that. The conspiracy still exists, still has power. If it isn't stopped, broken, they may still take control of the country."

"The answer is no," said Runner. "I am not coming aboard, Monaghan. I want no part of your group. Of you."

"You're thinkin' I used you, Jamie," he said, mildly. "And you're right. I'd use the Devil himself, if it gave me the slightest edge on these people. They've got to be stopped. We're the only ones who can do it."

He looked around the office again. "Jamie, why don't you give up this nonsense? Stop playin' school. There's a place for you."

"No. *Nein. Nyet. Non.* How many languages do you want me to say it in? Get out, Monaghan. Go away. Leave me alone."

"I can sympathize with what you're thinkin'," said the agent. "But we both know you're makin' a big mistake." He stood, started to turn for the door. Then he looked back one final time. "Come back to life, Jamie."

Runner stared; after thirty seconds, Monaghan shrugged, and left. He listened to the fading footsteps until they were completely gone.

But Runner's thought probed outward, across the university, as far as he could reach. Monaghan was right. The conspiracy still existed. Olana had ordered

Sandy Blake's death, but only because other people gave her a reason.

Olana was dead, but those others still lived. That wasn't right. That had to change.

Runner knew there was no chance he would formally join up with Monaghan and his group. He was done with taking orders from men no better than the armies, the men, they opposed.

But America was at war. The free world was at war. The citizens continued in their normal ways, lived a normal life of pleasure, sex, work, never suspecting what happened in that estate in Westchester. Never knowing how close a puppet had come to taking the highest office of the country.

The conspiracy had to be stopped.

Monaghan would be back. He'd come back when he had another definite target for Runner, a problem that required Runner's special talents, abilities.

Runner wouldn't say no to the agent then.